He was a man of about forty-five, dressed in a dark, shabby suit. Bunch saw that his fingers were closed over what seemed to be a handkerchief he was holding tightly to his chest. All round the clenched hand there were splashes of a dry brown fluid which, Bunch guessed, was dry blood.

Up till now the man's eyes had been closed, but at this point they suddenly opened and fixed themselves on Bunch's face. His lips moved, and Bunch bent forward. It was only one word that he said:

"Sanctuary . . ."

"The champion deceiver of our time."
—NEW YORK TIMES

Berkley books by Agatha Christie

AGATHA CHRISTIE

DOUBLE SIN
and Other Stories

BERKLEY BOOKS, NEW YORK

This Berkley book contains the complete
text of the original hardcover edition.
It has been completely reset in a typeface
designed for easy reading and was printed
from new film.

DOUBLE SIN AND OTHER STORIES

A Berkley Book / published by arrangement with
Dodd, Mead & Company

PRINTING HISTORY
Dodd, Mead edition published 1961
Dell edition / June 1980
Berkley edition / April 1984

ISBN: 0-425-06781-5

A BERKLEY BOOK ® TM 757,375
Berkley Books are published by The Berkley Publishing Group,
200 Madison Avenue, New York, NY 10016.
The name "BERKLEY" and the stylized "B" with design
are trademarks belonging to Berkley Publishing Corporation.

PRINTED IN THE UNITED STATES OF AMERICA

10   9   8   7   6

Contents

DOUBLE SIN
and Other Stories

Double Sin

I had called in at my friend Poirot's rooms to find him sadly overworked. So much had he become the rage that every rich woman who had mislaid a bracelet or lost a pet kitten rushed to secure the services of the great Hercule Poirot. My little friend was a strange mixture of Flemish thrift and artistic fervor. He accepted many cases in which he had little interest owing to the first instinct being predominant.

He also undertook cases in which there was a little or no monetary reward sheerly because the problem involved interested him. The result was that, as I say, he was overworking himself. He admitted as much himself, and I found little difficulty in persuading him to accompany me for a week's holiday to that well-known South Coast resort, Ebermouth.

We had spent four very agreeable days when Poirot came to me, an open letter in his hand.

"*Mon ami*, you remember my friend Joseph Aarons, the theatrical agent?"

I assented after a moment's thought. Poirot's friends are so many and so varied, and range from dustmen to dukes.

"*Eh bien*, Hastings, Joseph Aarons finds himself at Charlock Bay. He is far from well, and there is a little affair that it seems is worrying him. He begs me to go over and see him. I think, *mon ami*, that I must accede to his request. He is a faithful friend, the good Joseph Aarons, and has done much to assist me in the past."

"Certainly, if you think so," I said. "I believe Charlock Bay is a beautiful spot, and as it happens I've never been there."

"Then we combine business with pleasure," said Poirot. "You will inquire the trains, yes?"

"It will probably mean a change or two," I said with a grimace. "You know what these cross-country lines are. To go from the South Devon coast to the North Devon coast is sometimes a day's journey."

However, on inquiry, I found that the journey could be accomplished by only one change at Exeter and that the trains were good. I was hastening back to Poirot with the information when I happened to pass the offices of the Speedy cars and saw written up:

Tomorrow. All-day excursion to Charlock Bay. Starting 8:30 through some of the most beautiful scenery in Devon.

I inquired a few particulars and returned to the hotel full of enthusiasm. Unfortunately, I found it hard to make Poirot share my feelings.

"My friend, why this passion for the motor coach? The train, see you, it is sure? The tires, they do not burst; the accidents, they do not happen. One is not incommoded by too much air. The windows can be shut and no drafts admitted.''

I hinted delicately that the advantage of fresh air was what attracted me most to the motor-coach scheme.

"And if it rains? Your English climate is so uncertain."

"There's a hood and all that. Besides, if it rains badly, the excursion doesn't take place."

"Ah!" said Poirot. "Then let us hope that it rains."

"Of course, if you feel like that and . . ."

"No, no, *mon ami*. I see that you have set your heart on the trip. Fortunately, I have my great coat with me and two mufflers." He sighed. "But shall we have sufficient time at Charlock Bay?"

"Well, I'm afraid it means staying the night there. You see, the tour goes round by Dartmoor. We have lunch at Monkhampton. We arrive at Charlock Bay about four o'clock, and the coach starts back at five, arriving here at ten o'clock."

"So!" said Poirot. "And there are people who do this for pleasure! We shall, of course, get a reduction of the fare since we do not make the return journey?"

"I hardly think that's likely."

"You must insist."

"Come now, Poirot, don't be mean. You know you're coining money."

"My friend, it is not the meanness. It is the business sense. If I were a millionaire, I would pay only what was just and right."

As I had foreseen, however, Poirot was doomed to fail in this respect. The gentleman who issued tickets at the Speedy office was calm and unimpassioned but adamant. His point was that we ought to return. He even implied that we ought to pay extra for the privilege of leaving the coach at Charlock Bay.

Defeated, Poirot paid over the required sum and left the office.

"The English, they have no sense of money," he grumbled. "Did you observe a young man, Hastings, who paid over the full fare and yet mentioned his intention of leaving the coach at Monkhampton?"

"I don't think I did. As a matter of fact . . ."

"You were observing the pretty young lady who booked No. 5, the next seat to ours. Ah! Yes, my friend, I saw you. And that is why when I was on the point of taking seats No. 13 and 14—which are in the middle and as well sheltered as it is possible to be— you rudely pushed yourself forward and said that 3 and 4 would be better."

"Really, Poirot," I said, blushing.

"Auburn hair—always the auburn hair!"

"At any rate, she was more worth looking at than an odd young man."

"That depends upon the point of view. To me, the young man was interesting."

Something rather significant in Poirot's tone made me look at him quickly. "Why? What do you mean?"

"Oh! Do not excite yourself. Shall I say that he interested me because he was trying to grow a mustache and as yet the result is poor." Poirot stroked his own magnificent mustache tenderly. "It is an art," he murmured, "the growing of the mustache! I have sympathy for all who attempt it."

It is always difficult with Poirot to know when he is serious and when he is merely amusing himself at one's expense. I judged it safest to say no more.

The following morning dawned bright and sunny. A really glorious day! Poirot, however, was taking no chances. He wore a woolly waistcoat, a mackintosh, a heavy overcoat, and two mufflers, in addition to wearing his thickest suit. He also swallowed two tablets of "Antigrippe" before starting and packed a further supply.

We took a couple of small suitcases with us. The pretty girl we had noticed the day before had a small suitcase, and so did the young man whom I gathered to have been the object of Poirot's sympathy. Otherwise, there was no luggage. The four pieces were stowed away by the driver, and we all took our places.

Poirot, rather maliciously, I thought, assigned me the outside place as "I had the mania for the fresh air" and himself occupied the seat next to our fair neighbor. Presently, however, he made amends. The man in seat 6 was a noisy fellow, inclined to be facetious and boisterous, and Poirot asked the girl in a low voice if she would like to change seats with him. She agreed gratefully, and, the change having been effected, she entered into conversation with us and we were soon all three chattering together merrily.

She was evidently quite young, not more than nineteen, and as ingenuous as a child. She soon confided to us the reason of her trip. She was going, it seemed, on business for her aunt who kept a most interesting antique shop in Ebermouth.

This aunt had been left in very reduced circumstances on the death of her father and had used her small capital and a houseful of beautiful things which her father had left to start in business. She had been extremely successful and had made quite a name for herself in the trade. This girl, Mary Durrant, had come to be with her aunt and learn the business and was very excited about it—much preferring it to the other alternative—becoming a nursery governess or companion.

Poirot nodded interest and approval to all this.

"Mademoiselle will be successful, I am sure," he said gallantly. "But I will give her a little word of advice. Do not be too trusting, mademoiselle. Everywhere in the world there are rogues and vagabonds, even it may be on this very coach of ours. One should always be on the guard, suspicious!"

She stared at him open-mouthed, and he nodded sapiently.

"But yes, it is as I say. Who knows? Even I who speak to you may be a malefactor of the worst description."

And he twinkled more than ever at her surprised face.

We stopped for lunch at Monkhampton, and, after a few words with the waiter, Poirot managed to secure us a small table for three close by the window. Outside, in a big courtyard, about twenty *char-a-bancs* were parked—*char-a-bancs* which had come from all over the county. The hotel dining room was full, and the noise was rather considerable.

"One can have altogether too much of the holiday spirit," I said with a grimace.

Mary Durrant agreed. "Ebermouth is quite spoiled in the summers nowadays. My aunt says it used to be quite different. Now one can hardly get along the pavements for the crowd."

"But it is good for business, mademoiselle."

"Not for ours particularly. We sell only rare and valuable things. We do not go in for cheap bric-abrac. My aunt has clients all over England. If they want a particular period table or chair, or a certain piece of china, they write to her, and, sooner or later, she gets it for them. That is what has happened in this case."

We looked interested and she went on to explain. A certain American gentleman, Mr. J. Baker Wood, was a connoisseur and collector of miniatures. A very valuable set of miniatures had recently come into the market, and Miss Elizabeth Penn—Mary's aunt—had purchased them. She had written to Mr. Wood describing the miniatures and naming a price. He had replied at once, saying that he was prepared to purchase if the miniatures were as represented and asking that someone should be sent with them for him to see where he was staying at Charlock Bay. Miss Durrant had accordingly been dispatched, acting as representative for the firm.

"They're lovely things, of course," she said. "But I can't imagine anyone paying all that money for them. Five hundred pounds! Just think of it! They're by Cosway. Is it Cosway I mean? I get so mixed up in these things."

Poirot smiled. "You are not yet experienced, eh, mademoiselle?"

"I've had no training," said Mary ruefully. "We weren't brought up to know about old things. It's a lot to learn."

She sighed. Then suddenly, I saw her eyes widen in surprise. She was sitting facing the window, and her glance now was directed out of that window, into the courtyard. With a hurried word, she rose from her seat and almost ran out of the room. She returned in a few moments, breathless and apologetic.

"I'm so sorry rushing off like that. But I thought I saw a man taking my suitcase out of the coach. I went flying after him, and it turned out to be his own. It's one almost exactly like mine. I felt like such a fool. It looked as though I were accusing him of stealing it."

She laughed at the idea.

Poirot, however, did not laugh. "What man was it, mademoiselle? Describe him to me."

"He had on a brown suit. A thin weedy young man with a very indeterminate mustache."

"Aha," said Poirot. "Our friend of yesterday, Hastings. You know this young man, mademoiselle. You have seen him before?"

"No, never. Why?"

"Nothing. It is rather curious—that is all."

He relapsed into silence and took no further part in the conversation until something Mary Durrant said caught his attention.

"Eh, mademoiselle, what is that you say?"

"I said that on my return journey I should have to be careful of 'malefactors,' as you call them. I believe Mr. Wood always pays for things in cash. If I have five hundred pounds in notes on me, I shall be worth some malefactor's attention."

She laughed but again Poirot did not respond. Instead, he asked her what hotel she proposed to stay at in Charlock Bay.

"The Anchor Hotel. It is small and not expensive, but quite good."

"So!" said Poirot. "The Anchor Hotel. Precisely where Hastings here has made up his mind to stay. How odd!"

He twinkled at me.

"You are staying long in Charlock Bay?" asked Mary.

"One night only. I have business there. You could not guess, I am sure, what my profession is, mademoiselle?"

I saw Mary consider several possibilities and reject them—probably from a feeling of caution. At last, she hazarded the suggestion that Poirot was a conjurer. He was vastly entertained.

"Ah! But it is an idea, that! You think I take the rabbits out of the hat? No, mademoiselle. Me, I am the opposite of a conjurer. The conjurer, he makes things disappear. Me, I make things that have disappeared, reappear." He leaned forward dramatically so as to give the words full effect. "It is a secret, mademoiselle, but I will tell you, I am a detective!"

He leaned back in his chair pleased with the effect he had created. Mary Durrant stared at him spellbound. But any further conversation was barred for the braying of various horns outside announced that the road monsters were ready to proceed.

As Poirot and I went out together I commented on the charm of our luncheon companion. Poirot agreed.

"Yes, she is charming. But, also rather silly?"

"Silly?"

"Do not be outraged. A girl may be beautiful and have auburn hair and yet be silly. It is the height of foolishness to take two strangers into her confidence as she has done."

"Well, she could see we were all right."

"That is imbecile, what you say, my friend. Anyone who knows his job—naturally he will appear 'all right.' That little one she talked of being careful

when she would have five hundred pounds in money
with her. But she has five hundred pounds with her
now.''

"In miniatures."

"Exactly. In miniatures. And between one and the
other, there is no great difference, *mon ami*."

"But no one knows about them except us."

"And the waiter and the people at the next table.
And, doubtless, several people in Ebermouth! Mademoiselle Durrant, she is charming, but, if I were Miss
Elizabeth Penn, I would first of all instruct my new
assistant in the common sense." He paused and then
said in a different voice: "You know, my friend, it
would be the easiest thing in the world to remove a
suitcase from one of those *char-a-bancs* while we
were all at luncheon.''

"Oh! Come, Poirot, somebody will be sure to
see.''

"And what would they see? Somebody removing
his luggage. It would be done in an open and aboveboard manner, and it would be nobody's business to
interfere.''

"Do you mean—Poirot, are you hinting— But
that fellow in the brown suit—it was his own suitcase?''

Poirot frowned. "So it seems. All the same, it is
curious, Hastings, that he should have not removed
his suitcase before, when the car first arrived. He has
not lunched here, you notice.''

"If Miss Durrant hadn't been sitting opposite the
window, she wouldn't have seen him," I said slowly.

"And since it was his own suitcase, that would not
have mattered," said Poirot. "So let us dismiss it
from our thoughts, *mon ami*.''

Nevertheless, when we had resumed our places and were speeding along once more, he took the opportunity of giving Mary Durrant a further lecture on the dangers of indiscretion which she received meekly enough but with the air of thinking it all rather a joke.

We arrived at Charlock Bay at four o'clock and were fortunate enough to be able to get rooms at the Anchor Hotel—a charming old-world inn in one of the side streets.

Poirot had just unpacked a few necessaries and was applying a little cosmetic to his mustache preparatory to going out to call upon Joseph Aarons when there came a frenzied knocking at the door. I called "Come in," and, to my utter amazement, Mary Durrant appeared, her face white and large tears standing in her eyes.

"I do beg your pardon—but—but the most awful thing has happened. And you did say you were a detective?" This to Poirot.

"What has happened, mademoiselle?"

"I opened my suitcase. The miniatures were in a crocodile dispatch case—locked, of course. Now, look!"

She held out a small square crocodile-covered case. The lid hung loose. Poirot took it from her. The case had been forced; great strength must have been used. The marks were plain enough. Poirot examined it and nodded.

"The miniatures?" he asked, though we both knew the answer well enough.

"Gone. They've been stolen. Oh! What shall I do?"

"Don't worry," I said. "My friend is Hercule

Poirot. You must have heard of him. He'll get them back for you if anyone can."

"Monsieur Poirot. The great Monsieur Poirot."

Poirot was vain enough to be pleased at the obvious reverence in her voice. "Yes, my child," he said. "It is I, myself. And you can leave your little affair in my hands. I will do all that can be done. But I fear—I much fear—that it will be too late. Tell me, was the lock of your suitcase forced also?"

She shook her head.

"Let me see it, please."

We went together to her room, and Poirot examined the suitcase closely. It had obviously been opened with a key.

"Which is simple enough. These suitcase locks are all much of the same pattern. *Eh, bien*, we must ring up the police and we must also get in touch with Mr. Baker Wood as soon as possible. I will attend to that myself."

I went with him and asked what he meant by saying it might be too late. "*Mon cher*, I said today that I was the opposite of the conjurer—that I make the disappearing things reappear—but suppose someone has been beforehand with me. You do not understand? You will in a minute."

He disappeared into the telephone box. He came out five minutes later looking very grave. "It is as I feared. A lady called upon Mr. Wood with the miniatures half an hour ago. She represented herself as coming from Miss Elizabeth Penn. He was delighted with the miniatures and paid for them forthwith."

"Half an hour ago—before we arrived here."

Poirot smiled rather enigmatically. "The Speedy cars are quite speedy, but a fast motor from say,

Monkhampton would get here a good hour ahead of them at least."

"And what do we do now?"

"The good Hastings—always practical. We inform the police, do all we can for Miss Durrant, and—yes, I think decidedly, we have an interview with Mr. J. Baker Wood."

We carried out this program. Poor Mary Durrant was terribly upset, fearing her aunt would blame her.

"Which she probably will," observed Poirot, as we set out for the Seaside Hotel where Mr. Wood was staying. "And with perfect justice. The idea of leaving five hundred pounds' worth of valuables in a suitcase and going to lunch! All the same, *mon ami*, there are one or two curious points about the case. That dispatch box, for instance, why was it forced?"

"To get out the miniatures."

"But was not that a foolishness? Say our thief is tampering with the luggage at lunch time under the pretext of getting out his own. Surely it is much simpler to open the suitcase, transfer the dispatch case unopened to his own suitcase, and get away, than to waste the time forcing the lock?"

"He had to make sure the miniatures were inside."

Poirot did not look convinced, but, as we were just being shown into Mr. Wood's suite, we had no time for more discussion.

I took an immediate dislike to Mr. Baker Wood.

He was a large vulgar man, very much overdressed and wearing a diamond solitaire ring. He was blustering and noisy.

Of course, he'd not suspected anything amiss? Why should he? The woman said she had the miniatures all right. Very fine specimens, too! Had he the numbers of the notes? No, he hadn't. And who was Mr.—er—Poirot, anyway, to come asking him all these questions?

"I will not ask you anything more, monsieur, except for one thing. A description of the woman who called upon you. Was she young and pretty?"

"No, sir, she was not. Most emphatically not. A tall woman, middle-aged, grey hair, blotchy complexion and a budding mustache. A siren? Not on your life."

"Poirot," I cried, as we took our departure. "A mustache. Did you hear?"

"I have the use of my ears, thank you, Hastings."

"But what a very unpleasant man."

"He has not the charming manner, no."

"Well, we ought to get the thief all right," I remarked. "We can identify him."

"You are of such a naive simplicity, Hastings. Do you not know that there is such a thing as an alibi?"

"You think he will have an alibi?"

Poirot replied unexpectedly: "I sincerely hope so."

"The trouble with you is," I said, "that you like a thing to be difficult."

"Quite right, *mon ami*. I do not like—how do you say it—the bird who sits!"

Poirot's prophecy was fully justified. Our traveling companion in the brown suit turned out to be a Mr. Norton Kane. He had gone straight to the Gorge Hotel at Monkhampton and had been there during the afternoon. The only evidence against him was that of Miss Durrant who declared that she had seen him getting out his luggage from the car while we were at lunch.

"Which in itself is not a suspicious act," said Poirot meditatively.

After that remark, he lapsed into silence and refused to discuss the matter any further, saying when I pressed him, that he was thinking of mustaches in general, and that I should be well advised to do the same.

I discovered, however, that he had asked Joseph Aarons—with whom he spent the evening—to give him every detail possible about Mr. Baker Wood. As both men were staying at the same hotel, there was a chance of gleaning some stray crumbs of information. Whatever Poirot learned, he kept to himself, however.

Mary Durrant, after various interviews with the police, had returned to Ebermouth by an early morning train. We lunched with Joseph Aarons, and, after lunch, Poirot announced to me that he had settled the theatrical agent's problem satisfactorily, and that we could return to Ebermouth as soon as we liked. "But not by road, *mon ami*; we go by rail this time."

"Are you afraid of having your pocket picked, or of meeting another damsel in distress?"

"Both those affairs, Hastings, might happen to me on the train. No, I am in haste to be back in Ebermouth, because I want to proceed with our case."

"Our case?"

"But, yes, my friend. Mademoiselle Durrant appealed to me to help her. Because the matter is now in the hands of the police, it does not follow that I am free to wash my hands of it. I came here to oblige an old friend, but it shall never be said of Hercule Poirot that he deserted a stranger in need!" And he drew himself up grandiloquently.

"I think you were interested before that," I said shrewdly. "In the office of cars, when you first caught sight of that young man, though what drew your attention to him I don't know."

"Don't you, Hastings? You should. Well, well, that must remain my little secret."

We had a short conversation with the police inspector in charge of the case before leaving. He had interviewed Mr. Norton Kane, and told Poirot in confidence that the young man's manner had not impressed him favorably. He had blustered, denied, and contradicted himself.

"But just how the trick was done, I don't know," he confessed. "He could have handed the stuff to a confederate who pushed off at once in a fast car. But that's just theory. We've got to find the car and the confederate and pin the thing down."

Poirot nodded thoughtfully.

"Do you think that was how it was done?" I asked him, as we were seated in the train.

"No, my friend, that was not how it was done. It was cleverer than that."

"Won't you tell me?"

"Not yet. You know—it is my weakness—I like to keep my little secrets till the end."

"Is the end going to be soon?"

"Very soon now."

We arrived in Ebermouth a little after six and Poirot drove at once to the shop which bore the name "Elizabeth Penn." The establishment was closed, but Poirot rang the bell, and presently Mary herself opened the door, and expressed surprise and delight at seeing us.

"Please come in and see my aunt," she said.

She led us into a back room. An elderly lady came forward to meet us; she had white hair and looked rather like a miniature herself with her pink-and-white skin and her blue eyes. Round her rather bent shoulders she wore a cape of priceless old lace.

"Is this the great Monsieur Poirot?" she asked in a low charming voice. "Mary has been telling me. I could hardly believe it. And you will really help us in our trouble. You will advise us?"

Poirot looked at her for a moment, then bowed.

"Mademoiselle Penn—the effect is charming. But you should really grow a mustache."

Miss Penn gave a gasp and drew back.

"You were absent from business yesterday, were you not?"

"I was here in the morning. Later I had a bad headache and went directly home."

"Not home, mademoiselle. For your headache you tried the change of air, did you not? The air of Charlock Bay is very bracing, I believe."

He took me by the arm and drew me toward the door. He paused there and spoke over his shoulder.

"You comprehend, I know everything. This little —farce—it must cease."

There was a menace in his tone. Miss Penn, her face ghastly white, nodded mutely. Poirot turned to the girl.

"Mademoiselle," he said gently, "you are young and charming. But participating in these little affairs will lead to that youth and charm being hidden behind prison walls—and I, Hercule Poirot, tell you that that will be a pity."

Then he stepped out into the street and I followed him, bewildered.

"From the first, *mon ami*, I was interested. When that young man booked his place as far as Monkhampton only, I saw the girl's attention suddenly riveted on him. Now why? He was not of the type to make a woman look at him for himself alone. When we started on that coach, I had a feeling that something would happen. Who saw the young man tampering with the luggage? Mademoiselle and mademoiselle only, and remember she chose that seat —a seat facing the window—a most unfeminine choice.

"And then she comes to us with the tale of robbery—the dispatch box forced which makes not the common sense, as I told you at the time.

"And what is the result of it all? Mr. Baker Wood has paid over good money for stolen goods. The miniatures will be returned to Miss Penn. She will sell them and will have made a thousand pounds instead of five hundred. I make the discreet inquiries and learn that her business is in a bad state—touch and go. I say to myself—the aunt and niece are in this together."

"Then you never suspected Norton Kane?"

"*Mon ami!* With that mustache? A criminal is either clean shaven or he has a proper mustache that can be removed at will. But what an opportunity for the clever Miss Penn—a shrinking elderly lady with a pink-and-white complexion as we saw her. But if she holds herself erect, wears large boots, alters her complexion with a few unseemly blotches and—crowning touch—adds a few sparse hairs to her upper lip. What then? A masculine woman, says Mr. Wood, and—'a man in disguise' say we at once."

"She really went to Charlock yesterday?"

"Assuredly. The train, as you may remember telling me, left here at eleven and got to Charlock Bay at two o'clock. Then the return train is even quicker— the one we came by. It leaves Charlock at four:five and gets here at six:fifteen. Naturally, the miniatures were never in the dispatch case at all. That was artistically forced before being packed. Mademoiselle Mary has only to find a couple of mugs who will be sympathetic to her charm and champion beauty in distress. But one of the mugs was no mug—he was Hercule Poirot!"

I hardly liked the inference. I said hurriedly:

"Then, when you said you were helping a stranger, you were willfully deceiving me. That's exactly what you were doing."

"Never do I deceive you, Hastings. I only permit you to deceive yourself. I was referring to Mr. Baker Wood—a stranger to these shores." His face darkened. "Ah! When I think of that imposition, that iniquitous overcharge; the same fare single to Charlock as return, my blood boils to protect the visitor! Not a pleasant man, Mr. Baker Wood, not, as you would say, sympathetic. But a visitor! And we visitors, Hastings, must stand together. Me, I am all for the visitors!"

Wasps' Nest

Out of the house came John Harrison and stood a moment on the terrace looking out over the garden. He was a big man with a lean, cadaverous face. His aspect was usually somewhat grim but when as now, the rugged features softened into a smile, there was something very attractive about him.

John Harrison loved his garden, and it had never looked better than it did on this August evening, summery and languorous. The rambler roses were still beautiful; sweet peas scented the air.

A well-known creaking sound made Harrison turn his head sharply. Who was coming in through the garden gate? In another minute, an expression of utter astonishment came over his face, for the dandified figure coming up the path was the last he expected to see in this part of the world.

"By all that's wonderful," cried Harrison. "Monsieur Poirot!"

It was, indeed, the famous Hercule Poirot whose

renown as a detective had spread over the whole world.

"Yes," he said, "it is I. You said to me once: 'If you are ever in this part of the world, come and see me.' I take you at your word. I arrive."

"And I'm delighted," said Harrison heartily. "Sit down and have a drink."

With a hospitable hand, he indicated a table on the veranda bearing assorted bottles.

"I thank you," said Poirot, sinking down into a basket chair. "You have, I suppose, no syrup? No, no, I thought not. A little plain soda water then—no whisky." And he added in a feeling voice as the other placed the glass beside him: "Alas: My mustaches are limp. It is this heat!"

"And what brings you into this quiet spot?" asked Harrison as he dropped into another chair. "Pleasure?"

"No, *mon ami*, business."

"Business? In this out-of-the-way place?"

Poirot nodded gravely. "But yes, my friend, all crimes are not committed in crowds, you know?"

The other laughed. "I suppose that was rather an idiotic remark of mine. But what particular crime are you investigating down here, or is that a thing I mustn't ask?"

"You may ask," said the detective. "Indeed, I would prefer that you asked."

Harrison looked at him curiously. He sensed something a little unusual in the other's manner. "You are investigating a crime, you say?" he advanced rather hesitatingly. "A serious crime?"

"A crime of the most serious there is."

"You mean . . ."

"Murder."

So gravely did Hercule Poirot say that word that Harrison was quite taken aback. The detective was looking straight at him and again there was something so unusual in his glance that Harrison hardly knew how to proceed. At last, he said: "But I have heard of no murder."

"No," said Poirot, "you would not have heard of it."

"Who has been murdered?"

"As yet," said Hercule Poirot, "nobody."

"What?"

"That is why I said you would not have heard of it. I am investigating a crime that has not yet taken place."

"But look here, that is nonsense."

"Not at all. If one can investigate a murder before it has happened, surely that is very much better than afterward. One might even—a little idea—prevent it."

Harrison stared at him. "You are not serious, Monsieur Poirot."

"But yes, I am serious."

"You really believe that a murder is going to be committed? Oh, it's absurd!"

Hercule Poirot finished the first part of the sentence without taking any notice of the exclamation.

"Unless we can manage to prevent it. Yes, *mon ami*, that is what I mean."

"We?"

"I said we. I shall need your cooperation."

"Is that why you came down here?"

Again Poirot looked at him, and again an indefinable something made Harrison uneasy.

"I came here, Monsieur Harrison because I—well —like you."

And then he added in an entirely different voice: "I see, Monsieur Harrison, that you have a wasps' nest there. You should destroy it."

The change of subject made Harrison frown in a puzzled way. He followed Poirot's glance and said in rather a bewildered voice: "As a matter of fact, I'm going to. Or rather, young Langton is. You remember Claude Langton? He was at the same dinner where I met you. He's coming over this evening to take the nest. Rather fancies himself at the job."

"Ah!" said Poirot. "And how is he going to do it?"

"Petrol and the garden syringe. He's bringing his own syringe over; it's a more convenient size than mine."

"There is another way, is there not?" asked Poirot. "With cyanide of potassium?"

Harrison looked a little surprised. "Yes, but that's rather dangerous stuff. Always a bit of risk having it about the place."

Poirot nodded gravely. "Yes, it is deadly poison." He waited a minute and then repeated in a grave voice. "Deadly poison."

"Useful if you want to do away with your mother-in-law, eh?" said Harrison with a laugh.

But Hercule Poirot remained grave. "And you are quite sure, Monsieur Harrison, that it is with petrol that Monsieur Langton is going to destroy your wasps' nest?"

"Quite sure. Why?"

"I wondered. I was at the chemist's in Barchester this afternoon. For one of my purchases I had to sign the poison book. I saw the last entry. It was for cyanide of potassium and it was signed for by Claude Langton.''

Harrison stared. ''That's odd,'' he said. ''Langton told me the other day that he'd never dream of using the stuff; in fact, he said it oughtn't to be sold for the purpose.''

Poirot looked out over the roses. His voice was very quiet as he asked a question. ''Do you like Langton?''

The other started. The question somehow seemed to find him quite unprepared. ''I—I—well, I mean—of course, I like him. Why shouldn't I?''

''I only wondered,'' said Poirot placidly, ''whether you did.''

And as the other did not answer, he went on. ''I also wondered if he liked you?''

''What are you getting at, Monsieur Poirot? There's something in your mind I can't fathom.''

''I am going to be very frank. You are engaged to be married, Monsieur Harrison. I know Miss Molly Deane. She is a very charming, a very beautiful girl. Before she was engaged to you, she was engaged to Claude Langton. She threw him over for you.''

Harrison nodded.

''I do not ask what her reasons were; she may have been justified. But I tell you this, it is not too much to suppose that Langton has not forgotten or forgiven.''

''You're wrong, Monsieur Poirot. I swear you're wrong. Langton's been a sportsman; he's taken things like a man. He's been amazingly decent to me —gone out of his way to be friendly.''

''And that does not strike you as unusual? You use

the word 'amazingly,' but you do not seem to be amazed."

"What do you mean, M. Poirot?"

"I mean," said Poirot, and his voice had a new note in it, "that a man may conceal his hate till the proper time comes."

"Hate?" Harrison shook his head and laughed.

"The English are very stupid," said Poirot. "They think that they can deceive anyone but that no one can deceive them. The sportsman—the good fellow—never will they believe evil of him. And because they are brave, but stupid, sometimes they die when they need not die."

"You are warning me," said Harrison in a low voice. "I see it now—what has puzzled me all along. You are warning me against Claude Langton. You came here today to warn me . . ."

Poirot nodded. Harrison sprang up suddenly. "But you are mad, Monsieur Poirot. This is England. Things don't happen like that here. Disappointed suitors don't go about stabbing people in the back and poisoning them. And you're wrong about Langton. That chap wouldn't hurt a fly."

"The lives of flies are not my concern," said Poirot placidly. "And although you say Monsieur Langton would not take the life of one, yet you forget that he is even now preparing to take the lives of several thousand wasps."

Harrison did not at once reply. The little detective in his turn sprang to his feet. He advanced to his friend and laid a hand on his shoulder. So agitated was he that he almost shook the big man, and, as he did so, he hissed into his ear: "Rouse yourself, my friend, rouse yourself. And look—look where I am pointing. There on the bank, close by that tree root. See you, the wasps returning home, placid at the end of the day? In a little hour, there will be destruction, and they know it not. There is no one to tell them. They have not, it seems, a Hercule Poirot. I tell you, Monsieur Harrison, I am down here on business. Murder is my business. And it is my business before it has happened as well as afterward. At what time does Monsieur Langton come to take this wasps' nest?"

"Langton would never . . ."

"At what time?"

"At nine o'clock. But I tell you, you're all wrong. Langton would never . . ."

"These English!" cried Poirot in a passion. He caught up his hat and stick and moved down the path, pausing to speak over his shoulder. "I do not stay to argue with you. I should only enrage myself. But you understand, I return at nine o'clock?"

Harrison opened his mouth to speak, but Poirot did not give him the chance. "I know what you would say: 'Langton would never,' et cetera. Ah, Langton would never! But all the same I return at nine o'clock. But, yes, it will amuse me—put it like that—it will amuse me to see the taking of a wasps' nest. Another of your English sports!"

He waited for no reply but passed rapidly down the path and out through the door that creaked. Once outside on the road, his pace slackened. His vivacity died down, his face became grave and troubled. Once he drew his watch from his pocket and consulted it. The hands pointed to ten minutes past eight. "Over three quarters of an hour," he murmured. "I wonder if I should have waited."

His footsteps slackened; he almost seemed on the point of returning. Some vague foreboding seemed to assail him. He shook it off resolutely, however, and continued to walk in the direction of the village. But his face was still troubled, and once or twice he shook his head like a man only partly satisfied.

It was still some minutes of nine when he once more approached the garden door. It was a clear, still evening; hardly a breeze stirred the leaves. There was, perhaps, something a little sinister in the stillness, like the lull before a storm.

Poirot's footsteps quickened ever so slightly. He was suddenly alarmed—and uncertain. He feared he knew not what.

And at that moment the garden door opened and Claude Langton stepped quickly out into the road. He started when he saw Poirot.

"Oh—er—good evening."

"Good evening, Monsieur Langton. You are early."

Langton stared at him. "I don't know what you mean."

"You have taken the wasps' nest?"

"As a matter of fact, I didn't."

"Oh!" said Poirot softly. "So you did not take the wasps' nest. What did you do then?"

"Oh, just sat and yarned a bit with old Harrison. I really must hurry along now, Monsieur Poirot. I'd no idea you were remaining in this part of the world."

"I had business here, you see."

"Oh! Well, you'll find Harrison on the terrace. Sorry I can't stop."

He hurried away. Poirot looked after him. A nervous young fellow, good looking with a weak mouth!

"So I shall find Harrison on the terrace," murmured Poirot. "I wonder." He went in through the garden door and up the path. Harrison was sitting in a chair by the table. He sat motionless and did not even turn his head as Poirot came up to him.

"Ah! *Mon ami*," said Poirot. "You are all right, eh?"

There was a long pause and then Harrison said in a queer, dazed voice, "What did you say?"

"I said—are you all right?"

"All right? Yes, I'm all right. Why not?"

"You feel no ill effects? That is good."

"Ill effects? From what?"

"Washing soda."

Harrison roused himself suddenly. "Washing soda? What do you mean?"

Poirot made an apologetic gesture. "I infinitely regret the necessity, but I put some in your pocket."

"You put some in my pocket? What on earth for?"

Harrison stared at him. Poirot spoke quietly and impersonally like a lecturer coming down to the level of a small child.

"You see, one of the advantages, or disadvantages, of being a detective is that it brings you into contact with the criminal classes. And the criminal classes, they can teach you some very interesting and curious things. There was a pickpocket once—I interested myself in him because for once in a way he has not done what they say he has done—and so I get him off. And because he is grateful he pays me in the only way he can think of—which is to show me the tricks of his trade.

"And so it happens that I can pick a man's pocket if I choose without his ever suspecting the fact. I lay one hand on his shoulder, I excite myself, and he feels nothing. But all the same I have managed to transfer what is in his pocket to my pocket and leave washing soda in its place.

"You see," continued Poirot dreamily, "if a man wants to get at some poison quickly to put in a glass, unobserved, he positively must keep it in his right-hand coat pocket; there is nowhere else. I knew it would be there."

He dropped his hand into his pocket and brought out a few white, lumpy crystals. "Exceedingly dangerous," he murmured, "to carry it like that—loose."

Calmly and without hurrying himself, he took from another pocket a wide-mouthed bottle. He slipped in the crystals, stepped to the table and filled up the bottle with plain water. Then carefully corking it, he shook it until all the crystals were dissolved. Harrison watched him as though fascinated.

Satisfied with his solution, Poirot stepped across to the nest. He uncorked the bottle, turned his head aside, and poured the solution into the wasps' nest, then stood back a pace or two watching.

Some wasps that were returning alighted, quivered a little and then lay still. Other wasps crawled out of the hole only to die. Poirot watched for a minute or two and then nodded his head and came back to the veranda.

"A quick death," he said. "A very quick death."

Harrison found his voice. "How much do you know?"

Poirot looked straight ahead. "As I told you, I saw Claude Langton's name in the book. What I did not tell you was that almost immediately afterward, I happened to meet him. He told me he had been buy-ing cyanide of potassium at your request—to take a wasps' nest. That struck me as a little odd, my friend, because I remember that at that dinner of which you spoke, you held forth on the superior merits of petrol and denounced the buying of cyanide as dangerous and unnecessary."

"Go on."

"I knew something else. I had seen Claude Lang-ton and Molly Deane together when they thought no one saw them. I do not know what lovers' quarrel it was that originally parted them and drove her into your arms, but I realized that misunderstandings were over and that Miss Deane was drifting back to her love."

"Go on."

"I knew something more, my friend. I was in Harley Street the other day, and I saw you come out of a certain doctor's house. I know that doctor and for what disease one consults him, and I read the ex-pression on your face. I have seen it only once or twice in my lifetime, but it is not easily mistaken. It was the face of a man under sentence of death. I am right, am I not?"

"Quite right. He gave me two months."

"You did not see me, my friend, for you had other things to think about. I saw something else on your face—the thing that I told you this afternoon men try

to conceal. I saw hate there, my friend. You did not
trouble to conceal it, because you thought there were
none to observe.''

"Go on," said Harrison.

"There is not much more to say. I came down
here, saw Langton's name by accident in the poison
book as I tell you, met him, and came here to you. I
laid traps for you. You denied having asked Langton
to get cyanide, or rather you expressed surprise at his
having done so. You were taken aback at first at my
appearance, but presently, you saw how well it would
fit in and you encouraged my suspicions. I knew
from Langton himself that he was coming at half
past eight. You told me nine o'clock, thinking I
should come and find everything over. And so I knew
everything.''

"Why did you come?" cried Harrison. "If only
you hadn't come!''

Poirot drew himself up. "I told you," he said,
"murder is my business.''

"Murder? Suicide, you mean.''

"No." Poirot's voice rang out sharply and clearly.
"I mean murder. Your death was to be quick and
easy, but the death you planned for Langton was the
worst death any man can die. He bought the poison;
he comes to see you, and he is alone with you. You
die suddenly, and the cyanide is found in your glass,
and Claude Langton hangs. That was your plan.''

Again Harrison moaned.

"Why did you come? Why did you come?''

"I have told you, but there is another reason. I
liked you. Listen, *mon ami*, you are a dying man;
you have lost the girl you loved, but there is one thing

that you are not: you are not a murderer. Tell me now: are you glad or sorry that I came?"

There was a moment's pause and then Harrison drew himself up. There was a new dignity in his face —the look of a man who has conquered his own baser self. He stretched out his hand across the table.

"Thank goodness you came," he cried. "Oh! Thank goodness you came."

The Theft of the Royal Ruby

"I regret exceedingly . . ." said M. Hercule Poirot.

He was interrupted. Not rudely interrupted. The interruption was suave, dexterous, persuasive rather than contradictory.

"Please don't refuse offhand, Monsieur Poirot. There are grave issues of State. Your cooperation will be appreciated in the highest quarters."

"You are too kind." Hercule Poirot waved a hand, "but I really cannot undertake to do as you ask. At this season of the year . . ."

Again Mr. Jesmond interrupted. "Christmas time," he said, persuasively. "An old-fashioned Christmas in the English countryside."

Hercule Poirot shivered. The thought of the English countryside at this season of the year did not attract him.

"A good old-fashioned Christmas!" Mr. Jesmond stressed it.

"Me—I am not an Englishman," said Hercule

Poirot. "In my country, Christmas, it is for the children. The New Year, that is what we celebrate."

"Ah," said Mr. Jesmond, "but Christmas in England is a great institution and I assure you at Kings Lacey you would see it at its best. It's a wonderful old house, you know. Why, one wing of it dates from the fourteenth century."

Again Poirot shivered. The thought of a fourteenth-century English manor house filled him with apprehension. He had suffered too often in the historic country houses of England. He looked round appreciatively at his comfortable modern flat with its radiators and the latest patent devices for excluding any kind of draught.

"In the winter," he said firmly, "I do not leave London."

"I don't think you quite appreciate, Monsieur Poirot, what a very serious matter this is." Mr. Jesmond glanced at his companion and then back at Poirot.

Poirot's second visitor had up to now said nothing but a polite and formal "How do you do." He sat now, gazing down at his well-polished shoes, with an air of the utmost dejection on his coffee-colored face. He was a young man, not more than twenty-three, and he was clearly in a state of complete misery.

"Yes, yes," said Hercule Poirot. "Of course the matter is serious. I do appreciate that. His Highness has my heartfelt sympathy."

"The position is one of the utmost delicacy," said Mr. Jesmond.

Poirot transferred his gaze from the young man to his older companion. If one wanted to sum up Mr. Jesmond in a word, the word would have been discretion. Everything about Mr. Jesmond was discreet. His well-cut but inconspicuous clothes, his agreeable, well-bred voice which rarely soared out of an agreeable monotone, his light-brown hair just thinning a little at the temples, his pale serious face. It seemed to Hercule Poirot that he had known not one Mr. Jesmond but a dozen Mr. Jesmonds in his time, all using sooner or later the same phrase—"a position of the utmost delicacy."

"The police," said Hercule Poirot, "can be very discreet, you know."

Mr. Jesmond shook his head firmly.

"Not the police," he said. "To recover the—er— what we want to recover will almost inevitably involve taking proceedings in the law courts and we know so little. We *suspect*, but we do not *know*."

"You have my sympathy," said Hercule Poirot again.

If he imagined that his sympathy was going to mean anything to his two visitors, he was wrong. They did not want sympathy, they wanted practical help. Mr. Jesmond began once more to talk about the delights of an English Christmas.

"It's dying out, you know," he said, "the real old-fashioned type of Christmas. People spend it at hotels nowadays. But an English Christmas with all the family gathered round, the children and their stockings, the Christmas tree, the turkey and plum pudding, the crackers. The snow-man outside the window . . ."

In the interests of exactitude, Hercule Poirot intervened.

"To make a snow-man one has to have the snow," he remarked severely. "And one cannot have snow to order, even for an English Christmas."

"I was talking to a friend of mine in the meteoro-
logical office only today," said Mr. Jesmond, "and
he tells me that it is highly probable there *will* be
snow this Christmas."

It was the wrong thing to have said. Hercule Poirot
shuddered more forcefully than ever.

"Snow in the country!" he said. "That would be
still more abominable. A large, cold, stone manor
house."

"Not at all," said Mr. Jesmond. "Things have
changed very much in the last ten years or so. Oil-
fired central heating."

"They have oil-fired central heating at Kings
Lacey?" asked Poirot. For the first time he seemed
to waver.

Mr. Jesmond seized his opportunity. "Yes, indeed," he said, "and a splendid hot water system.
Radiators in every bedroom. I assure you, my dear
Monsieur Poirot, Kings Lacey is comfort itself in the
winter time. You might even find the house *too*
warm."

"That is most unlikely," said Hercule Poirot.

With practiced dexterity Mr. Jesmond shifted his
ground a little.

"You can appreciate the terrible dilemma we are
in," he said, in a confidential manner.

Hercule Poirot nodded. The problem was, indeed,
not a happy one. A young potentate-to-be, the only
son of the ruler of a rich and important native State
had arrived in London a few weeks ago. His country
had been passing through a period of restlessness and
discontent. Though loyal to the father whose way of
life had remained persistently Eastern, popular opin-

ion was somewhat dubious of the younger generation. His follies had been Western ones and as such looked upon with disapproval.

Recently, however, his betrothal had been announced. He was to marry a cousin of the same blood, a young woman who, though educated at Cambridge, was careful to display no Western influences in her own country. The wedding day was announced and the young prince had made a journey to England, bringing with him some of the famous jewels of his house to be reset in appropriate modern settings by Cartier. These had included a very famous ruby which had been removed from its cumbersome old-fashioned necklace and had been given a new look by the famous jewelers. So far so good, but after this came the snag. It was not to be supposed that a young man possessed of much wealth and convivial tastes, should not commit a few follies of the pleasanter type. As to that there would have been no censure. Young princes were supposed to amuse themselves in this fashion. For the prince to take the girl friend of the moment for a walk down Bond Street and bestow upon her an emerald bracelet or a diamond clip as a reward for the pleasure she had afforded him would have been regarded as quite natural and suitable, corresponding in fact to the Cadillac cars which his father invariably presented to his favorite dancing girl of the moment.

But the prince had been far more indiscreet than that. Flattered by the lady's interest, he had displayed to her the famous ruby in its new setting, and had finally been so unwise as to accede to her request to be allowed to wear it—just for one evening!

The sequel was short and sad. The lady had retired

from their supper table to powder her nose. Time passed. She did not return. She had left the establishment by another door and since then had disappeared into space. The important and distressing thing was that the ruby in its new setting had disappeared with her.

These were the facts that could not possibly be made public without the most dire consequences. The ruby was something more than a ruby, it was a historical possession of great significance, and the circumstances of its disappearance were such that any undue publicity about them might result in the most serious political consequences.

Mr. Jesmond was not the man to put these facts into simple language. He wrapped them up, as it were, in a great deal of verbiage. Who exactly Mr. Jesmond was, Hercule Poirot did not exactly know. He had met other Mr. Jesmonds in the course of his career. Whether he was connected with the Home Office, the Foreign Office or some more discreet branch of public service was not specified. He was acting in the interests of the Commonwealth. The ruby must be recovered.

M. Poirot, so Mr. Jesmond delicately insisted, was the man to recover it.

"Perhaps—yes," Hercule Poirot admitted, "but you can tell me so little. Suggestion—suspicion—all that is not very much to go upon."

"Come now, Monsieur Poirot, surely it is not beyond your powers. Ah, come now."

"I do not always succeed."

But this was mock modesty. It was clear enough from Poirot's tone that for him to undertake a mission was almost synonymous with succeeding in it.

"His Highness is very young," Mr. Jesmond said. "It will be sad if his whole life is to be blighted for a mere youthful indiscretion."

Poirot looked kindly at the downcast young man. "It is the time for follies, when one is young," he said encouragingly, "and for the ordinary young man it does not matter so much. The good papa, he pays up; the family lawyer, he helps to disentangle the inconvenience; the young man, he learns by experience and all ends for the best. In a position such as yours, it is hard indeed. Your approaching marriage . . ."

"That is it. That is it exactly." For the first time words poured from the young man. "You see she is very, very serious. She takes life very seriously. She has acquired at Cambridge many very serious ideas. There is to be education in my country. There are to be schools. There are to be many things. All in the name of progress, you understand, of democracy. It will not be, she says, like it was in my father's time. Naturally she knows that I will have diversions in London, but not the scandal. No! It is the scandal that matters. You see it is very, very famous, this ruby. There is a long trail behind it, a history. Much bloodshed—many deaths!"

"Deaths," said Hercule Poirot thoughtfully. He looked at Mr. Jesmond. "One hopes," he said, "it will not come to that?"

Mr. Jesmond made a peculiar noise rather like a hen who has decided to lay an egg and then thought better of it.

"No, no, indeed," he said, sounding rather prim. "There is no question, I am sure, of anything of *that* kind."

"You cannot be sure," said Hercule Poirot. "Whoever has the ruby now, there may be others who want to gain possession of it, and who will not stick at a trifle, my friend."

"I really don't think," said Mr. Jesmond, sounding more prim than ever, "that we need enter into speculations of that kind. Quite unprofitable."

"Me," said Hercule Poirot, suddenly becoming very foreign, "me, I explore all the avenues, like the politicians."

Mr. Jesmond looked at him doubtfully. Pulling himself together, he said, "Well, I can take it that is settled, Monsieur Poirot? You will go to Kings Lacey?"

"And how do I explain myself there?" asked Hercule Poirot.

Mr. Jesmond smiled with confidence.

"That, I think, can be arranged very easily," he said. "I can assure you that it will all seem quite natural. You will find the Laceys most charming. Delightful people."

"And you do not deceive me about the oil-fired central heating?"

"No, no, indeed." Mr. Jesmond sounded quite pained. "I assure you you will find every comfort."

"*Tout confort moderne,*" murmured Poirot to himself, reminiscently. "*Eh bien,*" he said, "I accept."

The temperature in the long drawing-room at Kings Lacey was a comfortable sixty-eight as Hercule Poirot sat talking to Mrs. Lacey by one of the big mullioned windows. Mrs. Lacey was engaged in needlework. She was not doing *petit point* or embroidering flowers upon silk. Instead, she appeared to be engaged in the prosaic task of hemming dishcloths. As she sewed she talked in a soft reflective voice that Poirot found very charming.

"I hope you will enjoy our Christmas party here, Monsieur Poirot. It's only the family, you know. My granddaughter and a grandson and a friend of his and Bridget who's my great-niece, and Diana who's a cousin and David Welwyn who is a very old friend. Just a family party. But Edwina Morecombe said that that's what you really wanted to see. An old-fashioned Christmas. Nothing could be more old-fashioned than we are! My husband, you know, absolutely lives in the past. He likes everything to be just as it was when he was a boy of twelve years old, and used to come here for his holidays." She smiled to herself. "All the same old things, the Christmas tree and the stockings hung up and the oyster soup and the turkey—two turkeys, one boiled and one roast—and the plum pudding with the ring and the bachelor's button and all the rest of it in it. We can't have sixpences nowadays because they're not pure silver any more. But all the old desserts, the Elvas plums and Carlsbad plums and almonds and raisins, and crystallized fruit and ginger. Dear me, I sound like a catalogue from Fortnum and Mason!"

"You arouse my gastronomic juices, madame."

"I expect we'll all have frightful indigestion by tomorrow evening," said Mrs. Lacey. "One isn't used to eating so much nowadays, is one?"

She was interrupted by some loud shouts and whoops of laughter outside the window. She glanced out.

"I don't know what they're doing out there. Playing some game or other, I suppose. I've always been so afraid, you know, that these young people would be bored by our Christmas here. But not at all, it's just the opposite. Now my own son and daughter and their friends, they used to be rather sophisticated about Christmas. Say it was all nonsense and too much fuss and it would be far better to go out to a hotel somewhere and dance. But the younger generation seem to find all this terribly attractive. Besides," added Mrs. Lacey practically, "schoolboys and schoolgirls are always hungry, aren't they? I think they must starve them at these schools. After all, one does know children of that age each eat about as much as three strong men."

Poirot laughed and said, "It is most kind of you and your husband, madame, to include me in this way in your family party."

"Oh, we're both delighted, I'm sure," said Mrs. Lacey. "And if you find Horace a little gruff," she continued, "pay no attention. It's just his manner, you know."

What her husband, Colonel Lacey, had actually said was: "Can't think why you want one of these damned foreigners here cluttering up Christmas? Why can't we have him some other time? Can't stick foreigners! All right, all right, so Edwina Morecombe wished him on us. What's it got to do with *her*, I should like to know? Why doesn't *she* have him for Christmas?"

"Because you know very well," Mrs. Lacey had said, "that Edwina always goes to Claridge's."

Her husband had looked at her piercingly and said, "Not up to something, are you, Em?"

"Up to something?" said Em, opening very blue

eyes. "Of course not. Why should I be?"

Old Colonel Lacey laughed, a deep, rumbling laugh. "I wouldn't put it past you, Em," he said. "When you look your most innocent is when you *are* up to something."

Revolving these things in her mind, Mrs. Lacey went on: "Edwina said she thought perhaps you might help us. . . . I'm sure I don't know quite how, but she said that friends of yours had once found you very helpful in—in a case something like ours. I— well, perhaps you don't know what I'm talking about?"

Poirot looked at her encouragingly. Mrs. Lacey was close on seventy, as upright as a ramrod, with snow-white hair, pink cheeks, blue eyes, a ridiculous nose and a determined chin.

"If there is anything I can do I shall only be too happy to do it," said Poirot. "It is, I understand, a rather unfortunate matter of a young girl's infatuation."

Mrs. Lacey nodded. "Yes. It seems extraordinary that I should—well, want to talk to you about it. After all, you *are* a perfect stranger. . . ."

"*And* a foreigner," said Poirot, in an understanding manner.

"Yes," said Mrs. Lacey, "but perhaps that makes it easier, in a way. Anyhow, Edwina seemed to think that you might perhaps know something—how shall I put it—something useful about this young Desmond Lee-Wortley."

Poirot paused a moment to admire the ingenuity of Mr. Jesmond and the ease with which he had made use of Lady Morecombe to further his own purposes.

"He has not, I understand, a very good reputation, this young man?'' he began delicately.

"No, indeed, he hasn't! A very bad reputation! But that's no help so far as Sarah is concerned. It's never any good, is it, telling young girls that men have a bad reputation? It—it just spurs them on!''

"You are so very right," said Poirot.

"In my young day," went on Mrs. Lacey. ("Oh dear, that's a very long time ago!) We used to be warned, you know, against certain young men, and of course it *did* heighten one's interest in them, and if one could possibly manage to dance with them, or to be alone with them in a dark conservatory . . ." she laughed. "That's why I wouldn't let Horace do any of the things he wanted to do.''

"Tell me," said Poirot, "exactly what it is that troubles you?''

"Our son was killed in the war," said Mrs. Lacey. "My daughter-in-law died when Sarah was born so that she has always been with us, and we've brought her up. Perhaps we've brought her up unwisely—I don't know. But we thought we ought always to leave her as free as possible.''

"That is desirable, I think," said Poirot. "One cannot go against the spirit of the times.''

"No," said Mrs. Lacey, "that's just what I felt about it. And, of course, girls nowadays do do these sort of things.''

Poirot looked at her inquiringly.

"I think the way one expresses it," said Mrs. Lacey, "is that Sarah has got in with what they call the coffeebar set. She won't go to dances or come out properly or be a deb or anything of that kind. Instead she has two rather unpleasant rooms in Chelsea down by the river and wears these funny clothes that they like to wear, and black stockings or bright green ones. Very thick stockings. (So prickly, I always think!) And she goes about without washing or combing her hair.''

"Ça, c'est tout à fait naturelle," said Poirot. "It is the fashion of the moment. They grow out of it.''

"Yes, I know,'' said Mrs. Lacey. "I wouldn't worry about *that* sort of thing. But you see she's taken up with this Desmond Lee-Wortley and he really has a *very* unsavory reputation. He lives more or less on well-to-do girls. They seem to go quite mad about him. He very nearly married the Hope girl, but her people got her made a ward in court or something. And of course that's what Horace wants to do. He says he must do it for her protection. But I don't think it's really a good idea, Monsieur Poirot. I mean, they'll just run away together and go to Scotland or Ireland or the Argentine or somewhere and either get married or else live together without getting married. And although it may be contempt of court and all that—well, it isn't really an answer, is it, in the end? Especially if a baby's coming. One has to give in then, and let them get married. And then, nearly always, it seems to me, after a year or two there's a divorce. And then the girl comes home and usually after a year or two she marries someone so nice he's almost dull and settles down. But it's particularly sad, it seems to me, if there is a child, because it's not the same thing, being brought up by a stepfather, however nice. No, I think it's much better if we did as we did in my young days. I mean the first young man one fell in love with was *always* someone undesirable. I remember I had a horrible passion for a young man called—now what was his name now?—how strange it is, I can't remember his Christian name at all! Tibbitt, that was his surname. Young Tibbitt. Of course, my father more or less forbade him the house, but he used to get asked to the same dances, and we used to dance together. And sometimes we'd escape and sit out together and occasionally friends would arrange picnics to which we both went. Of course, it was all very exciting and forbidden and one enjoyed it enormously. But one didn't go to the—well, to the *lengths* that girls go nowadays. And so, after a while, the Mr. Tibbitts faded out. And do you know, when I saw him four years later I was surprised what I could *ever* have seen in him! He seemed to be such a *dull* young man. Flashy, you know. No interesting conversation.''

"One always thinks the days of one's own youth are best," said Poirot, somewhat sententiously.

"I know," said Mrs. Lacey. "It's tiresome, isn't it? I mustn't be tiresome. But all the same I *don't* want Sarah, who's a dear girl really, to marry Desmond Lee-Wortley. She and David Welwyn, who is staying here, were always such friends and so fond of each other, and we did hope, Horace and I, that they would grow up and marry. But of course she just finds him dull now, and she's absolutely infatuated with Desmond."

"I do not quite understand, madame," said Poirot. "You have him here now, staying in the house, this Desmond Lee-Wortley?"

"That's *my* doing," said Mrs. Lacey. "Horace was all for forbidding her to see him and all that. Of course, in Horace's day, the father or guardian would have called round at the young man's lodgings with a horse whip! Horace was all for forbidding the fellow the house, and forbidding the girl to see him. I told him that was quite the wrong attitude to take. 'No,' I said. 'Ask him down here. We'll have him down for Christmas with the family party.' Of course, my husband said I was mad! But I said, 'At any rate, dear, let's *try* it. Let her see him in *our* atmosphere and *our* house and we'll be very nice to him and very polite, and perhaps then he'll seem less interesting to her'!"

"I think, as they say, you *have* something there, madame," said Poirot. "I think your point of view is very wise. Wiser than your husband's."

"Well, I hope it is," said Mrs. Lacey doubtfully. "It doesn't seem to be working much yet. But of course he's only been here a couple of days." A sudden dimple showed in her wrinkled cheek. "I'll confess something to you, Monsieur Poirot. I myself can't help liking him. I don't mean I *really* like him, with my *mind*, but I can feel the charm all right. Oh yes, I can see what Sarah sees in him. But I'm an old enough woman and have enough experience to know that he's absolutely no good. Even if I *do* enjoy his company. Though I do think," added Mrs. Lacey, rather wistfully, "he has *some* good points. He asked if he might bring his sister here, you know. She's had an operation and was in hospital. He said it was so sad for her being in a nursing home over Christmas and he wondered if it would be too much trouble if he could bring her with him. He said he'd take all her meals up to her and all that. Well now, I do think that *was* rather nice of him, don't you, Monsieur Poirot?"

"It shows a consideration," said Poirot, thoughtfully, "which seems almost out of character."

"Oh, I don't know. You can have family affections at the same time as wishing to prey on a rich

young girl. Sarah will be *very* rich, you know, not
only with what we leave her—and of course that
won't be very much because most of the money goes
with the place to Colin, my grandson. But her mother
was a very rich woman and Sarah will inherit all her
money when she's twenty-one. She's only twenty
now. No, I do think it was nice of Desmond to mind
about his sister. And he didn't pretend she was anything very wonderful or that. She's a shorthand typ-
ist, I gather—does secretarial work in London. And
he's been as good as his word and does carry up trays
to her. Not all the time, of course, but quite often. So
I think he has some nice points. But all the same,"
said Mrs. Lacey with great decision, "I don't want
Sarah to marry him."

"From all I have heard and been told," said
Poirot, "that would indeed be a disaster."

"Do you think it would be possible for you to help
us in any way?" asked Mrs. Lacey.

"I think it is possible, yes," said Hercule Poirot,
"but I do not wish to promise too much. For the Mr.
Desmond Lee-Wortleys of this world are clever,
madame. But do not despair. One can, perhaps, do a
little something. I shall at any rate, put forth my best
endeavors, if only in gratitude for your kindness in
asking me here for this Christmas festivity." He
looked round him. "And it cannot be so easy these
days to have Christmas festivities."

"No, indeed," Mrs. Lacey sighed. She leaned forward. "Do you know, Monsieur Poirot, what I really
dream of—what I would love to have?"

"But tell me, madame."

"I simply long to have a small, modern bungalow.
No, perhaps not a bungalow exactly, but a small,

modern, easy to run house built somewhere in the park here, and live in it with an absolutely up-to-date kitchen and no long passages. Everything easy and simple.''

''It is a very practical idea, madame.''

''It's not practical for me,'' said Mrs. Lacey. ''My husband *adores* this place. He *loves* living here. He doesn't mind being slightly uncomfortable, he doesn't mind the inconveniences and he would hate, simply *hate*, to live in a small modern house in the park!''

''So you sacrifice yourself to his wishes?''

Mrs. Lacey drew herself up. ''I do not consider it a sacrifice, Monsieur Poirot,'' she said. ''I married my husband with the wish to make him happy. He has been a good husband to me and made me very happy all these years, and I wish to give happiness to him.''

''So you will continue to live here,'' said Poirot.

''It's not really too uncomfortable,'' said Mrs. Lacey.

''No, no,'' said Poirot, hastily. ''On the contrary, it is most comfortable. Your central heating and your bath water are perfection.''

''We spent a lot of money in making the house comfortable to live in,'' said Mrs. Lacey. ''We were able to sell some land. Ripe for development, I think they call it. Fortunately right out of sight of the house on the other side of the park. Really rather an ugly bit of ground with no nice view, but we got a very good price for it. So that we have been able to have as many improvements as possible.''

''But the service, madame?''

''Oh, well, that presents less difficulty than you might think. Of course, one cannot expect to be looked after and waited upon as one used to be. Different people come in from the village. Two women in the morning, another two to cook lunch and wash it up, and different ones again in the evening. There are plenty of people who want to come and work for a few hours a day. Of course for Christmas we are very lucky. My dear Mrs. Ross always comes in every Christmas. She is a wonderful cook, really first-class. She retired about ten years ago, but she comes in to help us in any emergency. Then there is dear Peverell.''

"Your butler?''

"Yes. He is pensioned off and lives in the little house near the lodge, but he is so devoted, and he insists on coming to wait on us at Christmas. Really, I'm terrified, Monsieur Poirot, because he's so old and so shaky that I feel certain that if he carries anything heavy he will drop it. It's really an agony to watch him. And his heart is not good and I'm afraid of his doing too much. But it would hurt his feelings dreadfully if I did not let him come. He hems and hahs and makes disapproving noises when he sees the state our silver is in and within three days of being here, it is all wonderful again. Yes. He is a dear faithful friend.'' She smiled at Poirot. "So you see, we are all set for a happy Christmas. A white Christmas, too,'' she added as she looked out of the window. "See? It is beginning to snow. Ah, the children are coming in. You must meet them, Monsieur Poirot.''

Poirot was introduced with due ceremony. First, to Colin and Michael, the schoolboy grandson and his friend, nice polite lads of fifteen, one dark, one fair. Then to their cousin, Bridget, a black-haired girl of about the same age with enormous vitality.

"And this is my granddaughter, Sarah," said Mrs. Lacey.

Poirot looked with some interest at Sarah, an attractive girl with a mop of red hair; her manner seemed to him nervy and a trifle defiant, but she showed real affection for her grandmother.

"And this is Mr. Lee-Wortley."

Mr. Lee-Wortley wore a fisherman's jersey and tight black jeans; his hair was rather long and it seemed doubtful whether he had shaved that morning. In contrast to him was a young man introduced as David Welwyn, who was solid and quiet, with a pleasant smile, and rather obviously addicted to soap and water. There was one other member of the party, a handsome, rather intense looking girl who was introduced as Diana Middleton.

Tea was brought in. A hearty meal of scones, crumpets, sandwiches and three kinds of cake. The younger members of the party appreciated the tea. Colonel Lacey came in last, remarking in a noncommittal voice:

"Hey, tea? Oh yes, tea."

He received his cup of tea from his wife's hand, helped himself to two scones, cast a look of aversion at Desmond Lee-Wortley and sat down as far away from him as he could. He was a big man with bushy eyebrows and a red, weather-beaten face. He might have been taken for a farmer rather than the lord of the manor.

"Started to snow," he said. "It's going to be a white Christmas all right."

After tea the party dispersed.

"I expect they'll go and play with their tape recorders now," said Mrs. Lacey to Poirot. She looked indulgently after her grandson as he left the room. Her tone was that of one who says "The children are going to play with their toy soldiers."

"They're frightfully technical, of course," she said, "and very grand about it all."

The boys and Bridget, however, decided to go along to the lake and see if the ice on it was likely to make skating possible.

"*I* thought we could have skated on it this morning," said Colin. "But old Hodgkins said no. He's always so terribly careful."

"Come for a walk, David," said Diana Middleton, softly. David hesitated for half a moment, his eyes on Sarah's red head. She was standing by Desmond Lee-Wortley, her hand on his arm, looking up into his face.

"All right," said David Welwyn, "yes, let's."

Diana slipped a quick hand through his arm and they turned towards the door into the garden. Sarah said:

"Shall we go, too, Desmond? It's fearfully stuffy in the house."

"Who wants to walk?" said Desmond. "I'll get my car out. We'll go along to the Speckled Boar and have a drink."

Sarah hesitated for a moment before saying:

"Let's go to Market Ledbury to the White Hart. It's much more fun."

Though for all the world she would not have put it into words, Sarah had an instinctive revulsion from going down to the local pub with Desmond. It was, somehow, not in the tradition of Kings Lacey. The women of Kings Lacey had never frequented the bar of the Speckled Boar. She had an obscure feeling that to go there would be to let old Colonel Lacey and his wife down. And why not? Desmond Lee-Wortley would have said. For a moment of exasperation Sarah felt that he ought to know why not! One didn't upset such old darlings as Grandfather and dear old Em unless it was necessary. They'd been very sweet, really, letting her lead her own life, not understanding in the least why she wanted to live in Chelsea in the way she did, but accepting it. That was due to Em of course. Grandfather would have kicked up no end of a row.

Sarah had no illusions about her grandfather's attitude. It was not his doing that Desmond had been asked to stay at Kings Lacey. That was Em, and Em was a darling and always had been.

When Desmond had gone to fetch his car, Sarah popped her head into the drawing-room again.

"We're going over to Market Ledbury," she said. "We thought we'd have a drink there at the White Hart."

There was a slight amount of defiance in her voice, but Mrs. Lacey did not seem to notice it.

"Well, dear," she said, "I'm sure that will be very nice. David and Diana have gone for a walk, I see. I'm so glad. I really think it was a brainwave on my part to ask Diana here. So sad being left a widow so young—only twenty-two—I do hope she marries again *soon*."

Sarah looked at her sharply. "What are you up to, Em?"

"It's my little plan," said Mrs. Lacey gleefully. "I think she's just right for David. Of course I know he was terribly in love with *you*, Sarah dear, but you'd no use for him and I realize that he isn't your type. But I don't want him to go on being unhappy, and I think Diana will really suit him.''

"What a matchmaker you are, Em," said Sarah.

"I know," said Mrs. Lacey. "Old women always are. Diana's quite keen on him already, I think. Don't you think she'd be just right for him?"

"I shouldn't say so," said Sarah. "I think Diana's far too—well, too intense, too serious. I should think David would find it terribly boring being married to her."

"Well, we'll see," said Mrs. Lacey. "Anyway, *you* don't want him, do you, dear?"

"No, indeed," said Sarah, very quickly. She added, in a sudden rush, "You *do* like Desmond, don't you, Em?"

"I'm sure he's very nice indeed," said Mrs. Lacey.

"Grandfather doesn't like him," said Sarah.

"Well, you could hardly expect him to, could you?" said Mrs. Lacey reasonably, "but I dare say he'll come round when he gets used to the idea. You mustn't rush him, Sarah dear. Old people are very slow to change their minds and your grandfather *is* rather obstinate."

"I don't care what Grandfather thinks or says," said Sarah. "I shall get married to Desmond whenever I like!"

"I know, dear, I know. But do try and be realistic about it. Your grandfather could cause a lot of trouble, you know. You're not of age yet. In another year you can do as you please. I expect Horace will have come round long before that."

"You're on my side aren't you, darling?" said

Sarah. She flung her arms round her grandmother's neck and gave her an affectionate kiss.

"I want you to be happy," said Mrs. Lacey. "Ah! there's your young man bringing his car round. You know, I like these very tight trousers these young men wear nowadays. They look so smart—only, of course, it does accentuate knock knees."

Yes, Sarah thought, Desmond *had* got knock knees, she had never noticed it before. . . .

"Go on, dear, enjoy yourself," said Mrs. Lacey.

She watched her go out to the car, then, remembering her foreign guest, she went along to the library. Looking in, however, she saw that Hercule Poirot was taking a pleasant little nap, and smiling to herself, she went across the hall and out into the kitchen to have a conference with Mrs. Ross.

"Come on, beautiful," said Desmond. "Your family cutting up rough because you're coming out to a pub? Years behind the times here, aren't they?"

"Of course they're not making a fuss," said Sarah, sharply as she got into the car.

"What's the idea of having that foreign fellow down? He's a detective, isn't he? What needs detecting here?"

"Oh, he's not here professionally," said Sarah. "Edwina Morecombe, my godmother, asked us to have him. I think he's retired from professional work long ago."

"Sounds like a broken-down old cab horse," said Desmond.

"He wanted to see an old-fashioned English Christmas, I believe," said Sarah vaguely.

Desmond laughed scornfully. "Such a lot of tripe,

that sort of thing," he said. "How you can stand it I don't know."

Sarah's red hair was tossed back and her aggressive chin shot up.

"I enjoy it!" she said defiantly.

"You can't, baby. Let's cut the whole thing tomorrow. Go over to Scarborough or somewhere."

"I couldn't possibly do that."

"Why not?"

"Oh, it would hurt their feelings."

"Oh, bilge! You know you don't enjoy this childish sentimental bosh."

"Well, not really perhaps, but . . ." Sarah broke off. She realized with a feeling of guilt that she was looking forward a good deal to the Christmas celebration. She enjoyed the whole thing, but she was ashamed to admit that to Desmond. It was not the thing to enjoy Christmas and family life. Just for a moment she wished that Desmond had not come down there at Christmas time. In fact, she almost wished that Desmond had not come down here at all. It was much more fun seeing Desmond in London than here at home.

In the meantime the boys and Bridget were walking back from the lake, still discussing earnestly the problems of skating. Flecks of snow had been falling, and looking up at the sky it could be prophesied that before long there was going to be a heavy snowfall.

"It's going to snow all night," said Colin. "Bet you by Christmas morning we have a couple of feet of snow."

The prospect was a pleasurable one.

"Let's make a snow-man," said Michael.

"Good lord," said Colin, "I haven't made a snow-man since—well, since I was about four years old.''

"I don't believe it's a bit easy to do,'' said Bridget. "I mean, you have to know how.''

"We might make an effigy of Monsieur Poirot,'' said Colin. "Give it a big black moustache. There is one in the dressing-up box.''

"I don't see, you know,'' said Michael thoughtfully, "how Monsieur Poirot could ever have been a detective. I don't see how he'd ever be able to disguise himself.''

"I know,'' said Bridget, "and one can't imagine him running about with a microscope and looking for clues or measuring footprints.''

"I've got an idea,'' said Colin. "Let's put on a show for him!''

"What do you mean, a show?'' asked Bridget.

"Well, arrange a murder for him.''

"What a gorgeous idea,'' said Bridget. "Do you mean a body in the snow—that sort of thing?''

"Yes. It would make him feel at home, wouldn't it?''

Bridget giggled.

"I don't know that I'd go as far as that.''

"If it snows,'' said Colin, "we'll have the perfect setting. A body and footprints—we'll have to think that out rather carefully and pinch one of Grandfather's daggers and make some blood.''

They came to a halt and oblivious to the rapidly falling snow, entered into an excited discussion.

"There's a paintbox in the old schoolroom. We could mix up some blood—crimson-lake, I should think.''

"Crimson-lake's a bit too pink, *I* think,'' said Bridget. "It ought to be a bit browner.''

"Who's going to be the body?" asked Michael.

"I'll be the body," said Bridget quickly.

"Oh, look here," said Colin, "*I* thought of it."

"Oh, no, no," said Bridget, "it must be me. It's got to be a girl. It's more exciting. Beautiful girl lying lifeless in the snow."

"Beautiful girl! Ah-ha," said Michael in derision.

"I've got black hair, too," said Bridget.

"What's that got to do with it?"

"Well, it'll show up so well on the snow and I shall wear my red pajamas."

"If you wear red pajamas, they won't show the bloodstains," said Michael in a practical manner.

"But they'd look so effective against the snow," said Bridget, "and they've got white facings, you know, so the blood could be on that. Oh, won't it be gorgeous? Do you think he will really be taken in?"

"He will if we do it well enough," said Michael. "We'll have just your footprints in the snow and one other person's going to the body and coming away from it—a man's, of course. He won't want to disturb them, so he won't know that you're not really dead. You don't think," Michael stopped, struck by a sudden idea. The others looked at him. "You don't think he'll be *annoyed* about it?"

"Oh, I shouldn't think so," said Bridget, with facile optimism. "I'm sure he'll understand that we've just done it to entertain him. A sort of Christmas treat."

"I don't think we ought to do it on Christmas Day," said Colin reflectively. "I don't think Grandfather would like that very much."

"Boxing Day then," said Bridget.

"Boxing Day would be just right," said Michael.

"And it'll give us more time, too," pursued Bridget. "After all, there are a lot of things to arrange. Let's go and have a look at all the props."

They hurried into the house.

The evening was a busy one. Holly and mistletoe had been brought in in large quantities and a Christmas tree had been set up at one end of the dining-room. Everyone helped to decorate it, to put up the branches of holly behind pictures and to hang mistletoe in a convenient position in the hall.

"I had no idea anything so archaic still went on," murmured Desmond to Sarah with a sneer.

"We've always done it," said Sarah, defensively.

"What a reason!"

"Oh, don't be tiresome, Desmond. *I* think it's fun."

"Sarah my sweet, you *can't*!"

"Well, not—not really perhaps but—I do in a way."

"Who's going to brave the snow and go to midnight mass?" asked Mrs. Lacey at twenty minutes to twelve.

"Not me," said Desmond. "Come on, Sarah."

With a hand on her arm he guided her into the library and went over to the record case.

"There are limits, darling," said Desmond. "Midnight mass!"

"Yes," said Sarah. "Oh yes."

With a good deal of laughter, donning of coats and stamping of feet, most of the others got off. The two boys, Bridget, David and Diana set out for the ten minutes' walk to the church through the falling snow. Their laughter died away in the distance.

"Midnight mass!" said Colonel Lacey, snorting. "Never went to midnight mass in my young days. *Mass*, indeed! Popish, that is! Oh, I beg your pardon, Monsieur Poirot."

Poirot waved a hand. "It is quite all right. Do not mind me."

"Matins is good enough for anybody, I should say," said the colonel. "Proper Sunday morning service. 'Hark the herald angels sing,' and all the good old Christmas hymns. And then back to Christmas dinner. That's right, isn't it, Em?"

"Yes, dear," said Mrs. Lacey. "That's what *we* do. But the young ones enjoy the midnight service. And it's nice, really, that they *want* to go."

"Sarah and that fellow don't want to go."

"Well, there dear, I think you're wrong," said Mrs. Lacey. "Sarah, you know, *did* want to go, but she didn't like to say so."

"Beats me why she cares what that fellow's opinion is."

"She's very young, really," said Mrs. Lacey placidly. "Are you going to bed, Monsieur Poirot? Good night. I hope you'll sleep well."

"And you, madame? Are you not going to bed yet?"

"Not just yet," said Mrs. Lacey. "I've got the stockings to fill, you see. Oh, I know they're all practically grown up, but they do *like* their stockings. One puts jokes in them! Silly little things. But it all makes for a lot of fun."

"You work very hard to make this a happy house at Christmas time," said Poirot. "I honor you."

He raised her hand to his lips in a courtly fashion.

"Hm," grunted Colonel Lacey, as Poirot departed. "Flowery sort of fellow. Still—he appreciates you."

Mrs. Lacey dimpled up at him. "Have you noticed, Horace, that I'm standing under the mistletoe?" she asked with the demureness of a girl of nineteen.

Hercule Poirot entered his bedroom. It was a large room well provided with radiators. As he went over towards the big four poster bed he noticed an envelope lying on his pillow. He opened it and drew out a piece of paper. On it was a shakily printed message in capital letters.

DON'T EAT NONE OF THE PLUM PUDDING. ONE AS WISHES YOU WELL.

Hercule Poirot stared at it. His eyebrows rose. "Cryptic," he murmured, "and most unexpected."

Christmas dinner took place at two o'clock and was a feast indeed. Enormous logs crackled merrily in the wide fireplace and above their crackling rose the babel of many tongues talking together. Oyster soup had been consumed, two enormous turkeys had come and gone, mere carcasses of their former selves. Now, the supreme moment, the Christmas pudding was brought in, in state! Old Peverell, his hands and his knees shaking with the weakness of eighty years, permitted no one but himself to bear it in. Mrs. Lacey sat, her hands pressed together in nervous apprehension. One Christmas, she felt sure, Peverell would fall down dead. Having either to take the risk of letting him fall down dead or of hurting his feelings to such an extent that he would probably prefer to be dead than alive, she had so far chosen the former alternative. On a silver dish the Christmas pudding reposed in its glory. A large football of a pudding, a piece of holly stuck in it like a triumphant flag and glorious flames of blue and red rising round it. There was a cheer and cries of "Ooh-ah."

One thing Mrs. Lacey had done: prevailed upon Peverell to place the pudding in front of her so that she could help it rather than hand it in turn round the table. She breathed a sigh of relief as it was deposited safely in front of her. Rapidly the plates were passed round, flames still licking the portions.

"Wish, Monsieur Poirot," cried Bridget. "Wish before the flame goes. Quick, Gran darling, quick."

Mrs. Lacey leant back with a sigh of satisfaction. Operation Pudding had been a success. In front of everyone was a helping with flames still licking it. There was a momentary silence all round the table as everyone wished hard.

There was nobody to notice the rather curious expression on the face of Monsieur Poirot as he surveyed the portion of pudding on his plate. *"Don't eat none of the plum pudding."* What on earth did that sinister warning mean? There could be nothing different about his portion of plum pudding from that of everyone else! Sighing as he admitted himself baffled—and Hercule Poirot never liked to admit himself baffled—he picked up his spoon and fork.

"Hard sauce, Monsieur Poirot?"

Poirot helped himself appreciatively to hard sauce.

"Swiped my best brandy again, eh Em?" said the colonel good-humouredly from the other end of the table. Mrs. Lacey twinkled at him.

"Mrs. Ross insists on having the best brandy,

dear," she said. "She says it makes all the difference."

"Well, well," said Colonel Lacey, "Christmas comes but once a year and Mrs. Ross is a great woman. A great woman and a great cook."

"She is indeed," said Colin. "Smashing plum pudding, this. Mmmm." He filled an appreciative mouth.

Gently, almost gingerly, Hercule Poirot attacked his portion of pudding. He ate a mouthful. It was delicious! He ate another. Something tinkled faintly on his plate. He investigated with a fork. Bridget, on his left, came to his aid.

"You've got something, Monsieur Poirot," she said. "I wonder what it is."

Poirot detached a little silver object from the surrounding raisins that clung to it.

"Oooh," said Bridget, "it's the bachelor's button! Monsieur Poirot's got the bachelor's button!"

Hercule Poirot dipped the small silver button into the finger-bowl of water that stood by his plate, and washed it clear of pudding crumbs.

"It is very pretty," he observed.

"That means you're going to be a bachelor, Monsieur Poirot," explained Colin helpfully.

"That is to be expected," said Poirot gravely. "I have been a bachelor for many long years and it is unlikely that I shall change that status now."

"Oh, never say die," said Michael. "I saw in the paper that someone of ninety-five married a girl of twenty-two the other day."

"You encourage me," said Hercule Poirot.

Colonel Lacey uttered a sudden exclamation. His face became purple and his hand went to his mouth.

"Confound it, Emmeline," he roared, "why on earth do you let the cook put glass in the pudding?"

"Glass!" cried Mrs. Lacey, astonished.

Colonel Lacey withdrew the offending substance from his mouth. "Might have broken a tooth," he grumbled. "Or swallowed the damn' thing and had appendicitis."

He dropped the piece of glass into the finger-bowl, rinsed it and held it up.

"God bless my soul," he ejaculated. "It's a red stone out of one of the cracker brooches." He held it aloft.

"You permit?"

Very deftly Monsieur Poirot stretched across his neighbour, took it from Colonel Lacey's fingers and examined it attentively. As the squire had said, it was an enormous red stone the color of a ruby. The light gleamed from its facets as he turned it about. Somewhere around the table a chair was pushed back and then drawn in again.

"Phew!" cried Michael. "How wizard it would be if it was *real*."

"Perhaps it is real," said Bridget hopefully.

"Oh, don't be an ass, Bridget. Why a ruby of that size would be worth thousands and thousands and thousands of pounds. Wouldn't it, Monsieur Poirot?"

"It would indeed," said Poirot.

"But what *I* can't understand," said Mrs. Lacey, "is how it got into the pudding."

"Oooh," said Colin, diverted by his last mouthful, "I've got the pig. It isn't fair."

Bridget chanted immediately, "Colin's got the pig!

Colin's got the pig! Colin is the greedy guzzling *Pig*!''

"I've got the ring," said Diana in a clear, high voice.

"Good for you, Diana. You'll be married first, of us all."

"I've got the thimble," wailed Bridget.

"Bridget's going to be an old maid," chanted the two boys. "Yah, Bridget's going to be an old maid."

"Who's got the money?" demanded David. "There's a real ten shilling piece, gold, in this pudding. I know. Mrs. Ross told me so."

"I think I'm the lucky one," said Desmond Lee-Wortley.

Colonel Lacey's two next door neighbours heard him mutter, "Yes, you would be."

"*I've* got a ring, too," said David. He looked across at Diana. "Quite a coincidence, isn't it?"

The laughter went on. Nobody noticed that Monsieur Poirot carelessly, as though thinking of something else, had dropped the red stone into his pocket.

Mince-pies and Christmas dessert followed the pudding. The older members of the party then retired for a welcome siesta before the tea-time ceremony of the lighting of the Christmas tree. Hercule Poirot, however, did not take a siesta. Instead, he made his way to the enormous old-fashioned kitchen.

"It is permitted," he asked, looking round and beaming, "that I congratulate the cook on this marvelous meal that I have just eaten?"

There was a moment's pause and then Mrs. Ross came forward in a stately manner to meet him. She was a large woman, nobly built with all the dignity of a stage duchess. Two lean grey-haired women were beyond in the scullery washing up and a tow-haired girl was moving to and fro between the scullery and the kitchen. But these were obviously mere myrmidons. Mrs. Ross was the queen of the kitchen quarters.

"I am glad you enjoyed it, sir," she said graciously.

"Enjoyed it!" cried Hercule Poirot. With an extravagant foreign gesture he raised his hand to his lips, kissed it, and wafted the kiss to the ceiling. "But you are a genius, Mrs. Ross! A genius! *Never* have I tasted such a wonderful meal. The oyster soup . . ." he made an expressive noise with his lips. "—and the stuffing. The chestnut stuffing in the turkey, that was quite unique in my experience."

"Well, it's funny that you should say that, sir," said Mrs. Ross graciously. "It's a very special recipe, that stuffing. It was given me by an Austrian chef that I worked with many years ago. But all the rest," she added, "is just good, plain English cooking."

"And is there anything better?" demanded Hercule Poirot.

"Well, it's nice of you to say so, sir. Of course, you being a foreign gentleman might have preferred the continental style. Not but what I can't manage continental dishes, too."

"I am sure, Mrs. Ross, you could manage anything! But you must know that English cooking—*good* English cooking, not the cooking one gets in the second-class hotels or the restaurants—is much appreciated by *gourmets* on the continent, and I believe I am correct in saying that a special expedition was made to London in the early eighteen hundreds, and a report sent back to France of the wonders of the English puddings. 'We have nothing like that in France,' they wrote. 'It is worth making a journey to London just to taste the varieties and excellencies of the English puddings.' And above all puddings,'' continued Poirot, well launched now on a kind of rhapsody, ''is the Christmas plum pudding, such as we have eaten today. That was a home-made pudding, was it not? Not a bought one?''

"Yes, indeed, sir. Of my own making and my own recipe such as I've made for many, many years. When I came here Mrs. Lacey said that she'd ordered a pudding from a London store to save me the trouble. But no, madame, I said, that may be kind of you but no bought pudding from a store can equal a home-made Christmas one. Mind you,'' said Mrs. Ross, warming to her subject like the artist she was, ''it was made too soon before the day. A good Christmas pudding should be made some weeks before and allowed to wait. The longer they're kept, within reason, the better they are. I mind now that when I was a child and we went to church every Sunday, we'd start listening for the collect that begins 'Stir up O Lord we beseech thee' because that collect was the signal, as it were, that the puddings should be made that week. And so they always were. We had the collect on the Sunday, and that week sure enough my mother would make the Chrstmas puddings. And so it should have been here this year. As it was, that pudding was only made three days ago, the day before you arrived, sir. However, I kept to the old custom. Everyone in the house had to come out into the kitchen and have a stir and make a wish. That's an old custom, sir, and I've always held to it.''

"Most interesting," said Hercule Poirot. "Most interesting. And so everyone came out into the kitchen?"

"Yes, sir. The young gentlemen, Miss Bridget and the London gentleman who's staying here, and his sister and Mr. David and Miss Diana—Mrs. Middleton, I should say . . . All had a stir, they did."

"How many puddings did you make? Is this the only one?"

"No, sir, I made four. Two large ones and two smaller ones. The other large one I planned to serve on New Year's Day and the smaller ones were for Colonel and Mrs. Lacey when they're alone like and not so many in the family."

"I see, I see," said Poirot.

"As a matter of fact, sir," said Mrs. Ross, "it was the wrong pudding you had for lunch today."

"The wrong pudding?" Poirot frowned. "How is that?"

"Well, sir, we have a big Christmas mould. A china mould with a pattern of holly and mistletoe on top and we always have the Christmas Day pudding boiled in that. But there was a most unfortunate accident. This morning, when Annie was getting it down from the shelf in the larder, she slipped and dropped it and it broke. Well, sir, naturally I couldn't serve that, could I? There might have been splinters in it. So we had to use the other one—the New Year's Day one, which is in a plain bowl. It makes a nice round but it's not so decorative as the Christmas mould. Really, where we'll get another mould like that I don't know. They don't make things in that size nowadays. All tiddly bits of things. Why, you can't even buy a breakfast dish that'll take a proper eight to ten eggs and bacon. Ah, things aren't what they were."

"No, indeed," said Poirot. "But today that is not so. This Christmas Day has been like the Christmas Days of old, is that not true?"

Mrs. Ross sighed. "Well, I'm glad you say so, sir, but of course I haven't the *help* now that I used to have. Not skilled help, that is. The girls nowadays . . ." she lowered her voice slightly, "—they mean very well and they're very willing but they've not been *trained*, sir, if you understand what I mean."

"Times change, yes," said Hercule Poirot. "I, too, find it sad sometimes."

"This house, sir," said Mrs. Ross, "it's too large, you know, for the mistress and the colonel. The mistress, she knows that. Living in a corner of it as they do, it's not the same thing at all. It only comes alive, as you might say, at Christmas time when all the family come."

"It is the first time, I think, that Mr. Lee-Wortley and his sister have been here?"

"Yes, sir." A note of slight reserve crept into Mrs. Ross's voice. "A very nice gentleman he is but, well —it seems a funny friend for Miss Sarah to have, according to our ideas. But there—London ways are different! It's sad that his sister's so poorly. Had an operation, she had. She seemed all right the first day she was here, but that very day, after we'd been stirring the puddings, she was took bad again and she's been in bed ever since. Got up too soon after her operation, I expect. Ah, doctors nowadays, they have you out of hospital before you can hardly stand on your feet. Why, my very own nephew's wife . . ."

And Mrs. Ross went into a long and spirited tale of hospital treatment as accorded to her relations, comparing it unfavorably with the consideration that had been lavished upon them in older times.

Poirot duly commiserated with her. "It remains," he said, "to thank you for this exquisite and sumptuous meal. You permit a little acknowledgment of my appreciation?" A crisp five pound note passed from his hand into that of Mrs. Ross who said perfunctorily:

"You really shouldn't do *that*, sir."

"I insist. I insist."

"Well, it's very kind of you indeed, sir." Mrs. Ross accepted the tribute as no more than her due. "And I wish you, sir, a very happy Christmas and a prosperous New Year."

The end of Christmas Day was like the end of most Christmas Days. The tree was lighted, a splendid Christmas cake came in for tea, was greeted with approval but was partaken of only moderately. There was cold supper.

Both Poirot and his host and hostess went to bed early.

"Good night, Monsieur Poirot," said Mrs. Lacey. "I hope you've enjoyed yourself."

"It has been a wonderful day, madame, wonderful."

"You're looking very thoughtful," said Mrs. Lacey.

"It is the English pudding that I consider."

"You found it a little heavy, perhaps?" asked Mrs. Lacey delicately.

"No, no, I do not speak gastronomically. I consider its significance."

"It's traditional, of course," said Mrs. Lacey. "Well, good night, Monsieur Poirot, and don't dream too much of Christmas puddings and mince-pies."

"Yes," murmured Poirot to himself as he un-dressed. "It is a problem certainly, that Christmas plum pudding. There is here something that I do not understand at all." He shook his head in a vexed manner. "Well—we shall see."

After making certain preparations, Poirot went to bed, but not to sleep.

It was some two hours later that his patience was rewarded. The door of his bedroom opened very gently. He smiled to himself. It was as he had thought it would be. His mind went back fleetingly to the cup of coffee so politely handed him by Desmond Lee-Wortley. A little later, when Desmond's back was turned, he had laid the cup down for a few moments on a table. He had then apparently picked it up again and Desmond had had the satisfaction, if satisfaction it was, of seeing him drink the coffee to the last drop. But a little smile lifted Poirot's moustache as he reflected that it was not he but someone else who was sleeping a good sound sleep tonight. "That pleasant young David," said Poirot to himself, "he is worried, unhappy. It will do him no harm to have a night's really sound sleep. And now, let us see what will happen?"

He lay quite still, breathing in an even manner with occasionally a suggestion, but the very faintest suggestion, of a snore.

Someone came up to the bed and bent over him. Then, satisfied, that someone turned away and went to the dressing-table. By the light of a tiny torch the visitor was examining Poirot's belongings neatly arranged on top of the dressing-table. Fingers explored the wallet, gently pulled open the drawers of the dressing-table, then extended the search to the pockets of Poirot's clothes. Finally the visitor approached the bed and with great caution slid his hand under the pillow. Withdrawing his hand, he stood for a moment or two as though uncertain what to do next. He walked round the room looking inside ornaments, went into the adjoining bathroom from whence he presently returned. Then, with a faint exclamation of disgust, he went out of the room.

"Ah," said Poirot, under his breath. "You have a disappointment. Yes, yes, a serious disappointment. Bah! To imagine, even, that Hercule Poirot would hide something where you could find it!" Then, turning over on his other side, he went peacefully to sleep.

He was aroused next morning by an urgent soft tapping on his door.

"*Qui est là?* Come in, come in."

The door opened. Breathless, red-faced, Colin stood upon the threshold. Behind him stood Michael.

"Monsieur Poirot, Monsieur Poirot."

"But yes?" Poirot sat up in bed. "It is the early tea? But no. It is you, Colin. What has occurred?"

Colin was, for a moment, speechless. He seemed to be under the grip of some strong emotion. In actual fact it was the sight of the nightcap that Hercule Poirot wore that affected for the moment his organs of speech. Presently he controlled himself and spoke.

"I think—Monsieur Poirot, could you help us? Something rather awful has happened."

"Something has happened? But what?"

"It's—it's Bridget. She's out there in the snow. I think—she doesn't move or speak and—oh, you'd better come and look for yourself. I'm terribly afraid —she may be *dead*."

"What?" Poirot cast aside his bed covers. "Mademoiselle Bridget—dead!"

"I think—I think somebody's killed her. There's— there's blood and—oh do come!"

"But certainly. But certainly. I come on the instant."

With great practicality Poirot inserted his feet into his outdoor shoes and pulled a fur-lined overcoat over his pajamas.

"I come," he said. "I come on the moment. You have aroused the house?"

"No. No, so far I haven't told anyone but you. I thought it would be better. Grandfather and Gran aren't up yet. They're laying breakfast downstairs, but I didn't say anything to Peverell. She—Bridget— she's round the other side of the house, near the terrace and the library window."

"I see. Lead the way. I will follow."

Turning away to hide his delighted grin, Colin led the way downstairs. They went out through the side door. It was a clear morning with the sun not yet high over the horizon. It was not snowing now, but it had snowed heavily during the night and everywhere around was an unbroken carpet of thick snow. The world looked very pure and white and beautiful.

"There!" said Colin breathlessly. "I—it's— *there*!" He pointed dramatically.

The scene was indeed dramatic enough. A few

yards away Bridget lay in the snow. She was wearing scarlet pajamas and a white wool wrap thrown round her shoulders. The white wool wrap was stained with crimson. Her head was turned aside and hidden by the mass of her outspread black hair. One arm was under her body, the other lay flung out, the fingers clenched, and standing up in the center of the crimson stain was the hilt of a large curved Kurdish knife which Colonel Lacey had shown to his guests only the evening before.

"Mon Dieu!" ejaculated M. Poirot. "It is like something on the stage!"

There was a faint choking noise from Michael. Colin thrust himself quickly into the breach.

"I know," he said. "It—it doesn't seem *real* somehow, does it? Do you see those footprints—I suppose we mustn't disturb them?"

"Ah yes, the footprints. No, we must be careful not to disturb those footprints."

"That's what I thought," said Colin. "That's why I wouldn't let anyone go near her until we got you. I thought you'd know what to do."

"All the same," said Hercule Poirot briskly, "first, we must see if she is still alive? Is not that so?"

"Well—yes—of course," said Michael, a little doubtfully, "but you see, we thought—I mean, we didn't like . . ."

"Ah, you have the prudence! You have read the detective stories. It is most important that nothing should be touched and that the body should be left as it is. But we cannot be sure as yet if it *is* a body, can we? After all, though prudence is admirable, common humanity comes first. We must think of the doctor, must we not, before we think of the police?''

"Oh yes. Of course," said Colin, still a little taken aback.

"We only thought—I mean—we thought we'd better get you before we did anything," said Michael hastily.

"Then you will both remain here," said Poirot. "I will approach from the other side so as not to disturb these footprints. Such excellent footprints, are they not—so very clear? The footprints of a man and a girl going out together to the place where she lies. And then the man's footsteps come back but the girl's—do not."

"They must be the footprints of the murderer," said Colin, with bated breath.

"Exactly," said Poirot. "The footprints of the murderer. A long narrow foot with rather a peculiar type of shoe. Very interesting. Easy, I think, to recognize. Yes, those footprints will be very important."

At that moment Desmond Lee-Wortley came out of the house with Sarah and joined them.

"What on earth are you all doing here?" he demanded in a somewhat theatrical manner. "I saw you from my bedroom window. What's up? Good lord, what's this? It—it looks like . . ."

"Exactly," said Hercule Poirot. "It looks like murder, does it not?"

Sarah gave a gasp, then shot a quick suspicious glance at the two boys.

"You mean someone's killed the girl—what's-her-name—Bridget?" demanded Desmond. "Who on earth would want to kill her? It's unbelievable!"

"There are many things that are unbelievable,"

said Poirot. "Especially before breakfast, is it not? That is what one of your classics says. Six impossible things before breakfast." He added: "Please wait here, all of you."

Carefully making a circuit, he approached Bridget and bent for a moment down over the body. Colin and Michael were now both shaking with suppressed laughter. Sarah joined them, murmuring, "What have you two been up to?"

"Good old Bridget," whispered Colin. "Isn't she wonderful? Not a twitch!"

"I've never seen anything look so dead as Bridget does," whispered Michael.

Hercule Poirot straightened up again.

"This is a terrible thing," he said. His voice held an emotion it had not held before.

Overcome by mirth, Michael and Colin both turned away. In a choked voice Michael said:

"What—what must we do?"

"There is only one thing to do," said Poirot. "We must send for the police. Will one of you telephone or would you prefer me to do it?"

"I think," said Colin, "I think—what about it, Michael?"

"Yes," said Michael, "I think the jig's up now." He stepped forward. For the first time he seemed a little unsure of himself. "I'm awfully sorry," he said, "I hope you won't mind too much. It—er—it was a sort of joke for Christmas and all that, you know. We thought we'd—well, lay on a murder for you."

"You thought you would lay on a murder for me? Then this—then this . . ."

"It's just a show we put on," explained Colin, "to —to make you feel at home, you know."

"Aha," said Hercule Poirot. "I understand. You make of me the April fool, is that it? But today is not April the first, it is December the twenty-sixth."

"I suppose we oughtn't to have done it really," said Colin, "but—but—you don't mind very much, do you, Monsieur Poirot? Come on, Bridget," he called, "get up. You must be half-frozen to death already."

The figure in the snow, however, did not stir.

"It is odd," said Hercule Poirot, "she does not seem to hear you." He looked thoughtfully at them. "It is a joke, you say? You are sure this is a joke?"

"Why, yes." Colin spoke uncomfortably. "We— we didn't mean any harm."

"But why then does Mademoiselle Bridget not get up?"

"I can't imagine," said Colin.

"Come on, Bridget," said Sarah impatiently. "Don't go on lying there playing the fool."

"We really are very sorry, Monsieur Poirot," said Colin apprehensively. "We do really apologize."

"You need not apologize," said Poirot, in a peculiar tone.

"What do you mean?" Colin stared at him. He turned again. "Bridget! Bridget! What's the matter? Why doesn't she get up? Why does she go on lying there?"

Poirot beckoned to Desmond. "*You*, Mr. Lee-Wortley. Come here . . ."

Desmond joined him.

"Feel her pulse," said Poirot.

Desmond Lee-Wortley bent down. He touched the arm—the wrist.

"There's no pulse . . ." he stared at Poirot. "Her

arm's stiff. Good God, she really *is* dead!''

Poirot nodded. ''Yes, she is dead,'' he said. ''Someone has turned the comedy into a tragedy.''

''Someone—who?''

''There is a set of footprints going and returning. A set of footprints that bears a strong resemblance to the footprints *you* have just made, Mr. Lee-Wortley, coming from the path to this spot.''

Desmond Lee-Wortley wheeled round.

''What on earth . . . Are you accusing me? *ME?* You're crazy! Why on earth should I want to kill the girl?''

''Ah—why? I wonder . . . Let us see. . . .''

He bent down and very gently prised open the stiff fingers of the girl's clenched hand.

Desmond drew a sharp breath. He gazed down unbelievingly. In the palm of the dead girl's hand was what appeared to be a large ruby.

''It's that damn' thing out of the pudding!'' he cried.

''Is it?'' said Poirot. ''Are you sure?''

''Of course it is.''

With a swift movement Desmond bent down and plucked the red stone out of Bridget's hand.

''You should not do that,'' said Poirot reproachfully. ''Nothing should have been disturbed.''

''I haven't disturbed the body, have I? But this thing might—might get lost and it's evidence. The great thing is to get the police here as soon as possible. I'll go at once and telephone.''

He wheeled round and ran sharply towards the house. Sarah came swiftly to Poirot's side.

''I don't understand,'' she whispered. Her face was dead white. ''I don't *understand*.'' She caught at

Poirot's arm. "What did you mean about—about the footprints?"

"Look for yourself, mademoiselle."

The footprints that led to the body and back again were the same as the ones just made accompanying Poirot to the girl's body and back.

"You mean—that it was Desmond? Nonsense!"

Suddenly the noise of a car came through the clear air. They wheeled round. They saw the car clearly enough driving at a furious pace down the drive and Sarah recognized what car it was.

"It's Desmond," she said. "It's Desmond's car. He—he must have gone to fetch the police instead of telephoning."

Diana Middleton came running out of the house to join them.

"What's happened?" she cried in a breathless voice. "Desmond just came rushing into the house. He said something about Bridget being killed and then he rattled the telephone but it was dead. He couldn't get any answer. He said the wires must have been cut. He said the only thing was to take a car and go for the police. Why the police? . . ."

Poirot made a gesture.

"Bridget?" Diana stared at him. "But surely— isn't it a joke of some kind? I heard something— something last night. I thought that they were going to play a joke on you, Monsieur Poirot?"

"Yes," said Poirot, "that was the idea—to play a joke on me. But now come into the house, all of you. We shall catch our deaths of cold here and there is nothing to be done until Mr. Lee-Wortley returns with the police."

"But look here," said Colin, "we can't—we can't

leave Bridget here alone.''

"You can do her no good by remaining," said Poirot gently. "Come, it is a sad, a very sad tragedy, but there is nothing we can do any more to help Mademoiselle Bridget. So let us come in and get warm and have perhaps a cup of tea or of coffee.''

They followed him obediently into the house. Peverell was just about to ring the gong. If he thought it extraordinary for most of the household to be outside and for Poirot to make an appearance in pajamas and an overcoat, he displayed no sign of it. Peverell in his old age was still the perfect butler. He noticed nothing that he was not asked to notice. They went into the dining-room and sat down. When they all had a cup of coffee in front of them and were sipping it, Poirot spoke.

"I have to recount to you," he said, "a little history. I cannot tell you all the details, no. But I can give you the main outline. It concerns a young princeling who came to this country. He brought with him a famous jewel which he was to have reset for the lady he was going to marry, but unfortunately before that he made friends with a very pretty young lady. This pretty young lady did not care very much for the man, but she did care for his jewel—so much so that one day she disappeared with this historic possession which had belonged to his house for generations. So the poor young man, he is in a quandary, you see. Above all he cannot have a scandal. Impossible to go to the police. Therefore he comes to me, to Hercule Poirot. 'Recover for me,' he says, 'my historic ruby.' *Eh bien*, this young lady, she has a friend and the friend, he has put through several very questionable transactions. He has been concerned with blackmail and he has been concerned with the sale of jewelry abroad. Always he has been very clever. He is suspected, yes, but nothing can be proved. It comes to my knowledge that this very clever gentleman, he is spending Christmas here in this house. It is important that the pretty young lady, once she has acquired the jewel, should disappear for a while from circulation, so that no pressure can be put upon her, no questions can be asked her. It is arranged, therefore, that she comes here to Kings Lacey, ostensibly as the sister of the clever gentleman . . ."

Sarah drew a sharp breath.

"Oh, no. Oh, no, not *here*! Not with me here!"

"But so it is," said Poirot. "And by a little manipulation I, too, become a guest here for Christmas. This young lady, she is supposed to have just come out of hospital. She is much better when she arrives here. But then comes the news that I, too, arrive, a detective—a well-known detective. At once she has what you call the wind up. She hides the ruby in the first place she can think of, and then very quickly she has a relapse and takes to her bed again. She does not want that I should see her, for doubtless I have a photograph and I shall recognize her. It is very boring for her, yes, but she has to stay in her room and her brother, he brings her up the trays."

"And the ruby?" demanded Michael.

"I think," said Poirot, "that at the moment it is mentioned I arrive, the young lady was in the kitchen with the rest of you, all laughing and talking and stirring the Christmas puddings. The Christmas puddings are put into bowls and the young lady she hides the ruby, pressing it down into one of the pudding bowls. Not the one that we are going to have on Christmas Day. Oh no, that one she knows is in a special mould. She puts it in the other one, the one that is destined to be eaten on New Year's Day. Before then she will be ready to leave, and when she leaves no doubt that Christmas pudding will go with her. But see how fate takes a hand. On the very morning of Christmas Day there is an accident. The Christmas pudding in its fancy mould is dropped on the stone floor and the mould is shattered to pieces. So what can be done? The good Mrs. Ross, she takes the other pudding and sends it in."

"Good lord," said Colin, "do you mean that on Christmas Day when Grandfather was eating his pudding that that was a *real* ruby he'd got in his mouth?"

"Precisely," said Poirot, "and you can imagine the emotions of Mr. Desmond Lee-Wortley when he saw that. *Eh bien*, what happens next? The ruby is passed round. I examine it and I manage unobtrusively to slip it in my pocket. In a careless way as though I were not interested. But one person at least observes what I have done. When I lie in bed that person searches my room. He searches me. He does not find the ruby. Why?"

"Because," said Michael breathlessly, "you had given it to Bridget. That's what you mean. And so that's why—but I don't understand quite—I mean . . . Look here, what *did* happen?"

Poirot smiled at him.

"Come now into the library," he said, "and look out of the window and I will show you something that may explain the mystery."

He led the way and they followed him.

"Consider once again," said Poirot, "the scene of the crime."

He pointed out of the window. A simultaneous gasp broke from the lips of all of them. There was no body lying on the snow, no trace of the tragedy seemed to remain except a mass of scuffled snow.

"It wasn't all a dream, was it?" said Colin faintly. "I—has someone taken the body away?"

"Ah," said Poirot. "You see? The Mystery of the Disappearing Body." He nodded his head and his eyes twinkled gently.

"Good lord," cried Michael. "Monsieur Poirot, you are—you haven't—oh, look here, he's been having us on all this time!"

Poirot twinkled more than ever.

"It is true, my children, I also have had my little joke. I knew about your little plot, you see, and so I arranged a counter-plot of my own. Ah, *voilà* Mademoiselle Bridget. None the worse, I hope, for your exposure in the snow? Never should I forgive myself if you *attrapped une fluxion de poitrine.*"

Bridget had just come into the room. She was wearing a thick skirt and a woollen sweater. She was laughing.

"I sent a *tisane* to your room," said Poirot severely. "You have drunk it?"

"One sip was enough!" said Bridget. "*I*'m all right. Did I do it well, Monsieur Poirot? Goodness, my arm hurts still after that tourniquet you made me put on it."

"You were splendid, my child," said Poirot. "Splendid. But see, all the others are still in the fog. Last night I went to Mademoiselle Bridget. I told her that I knew about your little *complot* and I asked her if she would act a part for me. She did it very cleverly. She made the footprints with a pair of Mr. Lee-Wortley's shoes."

Sarah said in a harsh voice:

"But what's the point of it all, Monsieur Poirot? What's the point of sending Desmond off to fetch the police? They'll be very angry when they find out it's nothing but a hoax."

Poirot shook his head gently.

"But I do not think for one moment, Mademoiselle, that Mr. Lee-Wortley went to fetch the police," he said. "Murder is a thing in which Mr. Lee-Wortley does not want to be mixed up. He lost his nerve badly. All he could see was his chance to get the ruby. He snatched that, he pretended the telephone was out of order and he rushed off in a car on the pretence of fetching the police. I think myself it is the last you will see of him for some time. He has, I understand, his own ways of getting out of England. He has his own plane, has he not, mademoiselle?"

Sarah nodded. "Yes," she said. "We were thinking of . . ." She stopped.

"He wanted you to elope with him that way, did he not? *Eh bien*, that is a very good way of smuggling a jewel out of the country. When you are eloping with a girl, and that fact is publicized, then you will not be suspected of also smuggling a historic jewel out of the country. Oh yes, that would have made a very good *camouflage*."

"I don't believe it," said Sarah. "I don't believe a word of it!"

"Then ask his sister," said Poirot, gently nodding his head over her shoulder. Sarah turned her head sharply.

A platinum blonde stood in the doorway. She wore a fur coat and was scowling. She was clearly in a furious temper.

"Sister my foot!" she said, with a short unpleasant laugh. "That swine's no brother of mine! So he's beaten it, has he, and left me to carry the can? The whole thing was *his* idea! *He* put me up to it! Said it was money for jam. They'd never prosecute because of the scandal. I could always threaten to say that Ali had *given* me his historic jewel. Des and I were to have shared the swag in Paris—and now the swine runs out on me! I'd like to murder him!" She switched abruptly. "The sooner I get out of here . . . Can someone telephone for a taxi?"

"A car is waiting at the front door to take you to the station, mademoiselle," said Poirot.

"Think of everything, don't you?"

"Most things," said Poirot complacently.

But Poirot was not to get off so easily. When he returned to the dining-room after assisting the spurious Miss Lee-Wortley into the waiting car, Colin was waiting for him.

There was a frown on his boyish face.

"But look here, Monsieur Poirot. *What about the ruby?* Do you mean to say you've let him get away with it?"

Poirot's face fell. He twirled his moustaches. He seemed ill at ease.

"I shall recover it yet," he said weakly. "There are other ways. I shall still . . ."

"Well, I do think!" said Michael. "To let that swine get away with the ruby!"

Bridget was sharper.

"He's having us on again," she cried. "You are,

aren't you, Monsieur Poirot?''

"Shall we do a final conjuring trick, Mademoi-selle? Feel in my left-hand pocket.''

Bridget thrust her hand in. She drew it out again with a scream of triumph and held aloft a large ruby blinking in crimson splendor.

"You comprehend," explained Poirot, "the one that was clasped in your hand was a paste replica. I brought it from London in case it was possible to make a substitution. You understand? We do not want the scandal. Monsieur Desmond will try and dispose of that ruby in Paris or in Belgium or wher-ever it is that he has his contacts, and then it will be discovered that the stone is not real! What could be more excellent? All finishes happily. The scandal is avoided, my princeling receives his ruby back again, he returns to his country and makes a sober and we hope a happy marriage. All ends well.''

"Except for me,'' murmured Sarah under her breath.

She spoke so low that no one heard her but Poirot. He shook his head gently.

"You are in error, Mademoiselle Sarah, in what you say there. You have gained experience. All expe-rience is valuable. Ahead of you I prophesy there lies happiness.''

"That's what *you* say,'' said Sarah.

"But look here, Monsieur Poirot," Colin was frowning. "How did you know about the show we were going to put on for you?''

"It is my business to know things," said Hercule Poirot. He twirled his moustache.

"Yes, but I don't see how you could have managed

it. Did someone split—did someone come and tell you?"

"No, no, not that."

"Then how? Tell us how?"

They all chorused, "Yes, tell us how."

"But no," Poirot protested. "But not. If I tell you how I deduced that, you will think nothing of it. It is like the conjuror who shows how his tricks are done!"

"Tell us, Monsieur Poirot! Go on. Tell us, tell us!"

"You really wish that I should solve for you this last mystery?"

"Yes, go on. Tell us."

"Ah, I do not think I can. You will be so disappointed."

"Now, come on, Monsieur Poirot, tell us. *How did you know?*"

"Well, you see, I was sitting in the library by the window in a chair after tea the other day and I was reposing myself. I had been asleep and when I awoke you were discussing your plans just outside the window close to me, and the window was open at the top."

"Is that all?" cried Colin, disgusted. "How simple!"

"Is it not?" cried Hercule Poirot, smiling. "You see? You *are* disappointed!"

"Oh well," said Michael, "at any rate we know everything now."

"Do we?" murmured Hercule Poirot to himself. "*I* do not. *I*, whose business it is to know things."

He walked out into the hall, shaking his head a

little. For perhaps the twentieth time he drew from
his pocket a rather dirty piece of paper. "DON'T
EAT NONE OF THE PLUM PUDDING. ONE AS
WISHES YOU WELL."

Hercule Poirot shook his head reflectively. He who
could explain everything could not explain this!
Humiliating. Who had written it? *Why* had it been
written? Until he found that out he would never
know a moment's peace. Suddenly he came out of his
reverie to be aware of a peculiar gasping noise. He
looked sharply down. On the floor, busy with a dust-
pan and brush was a tow-headed creature in a flow-
ered overall. She was staring at the paper in his hand
with large round eyes.

"Oh sir," said this apparition. "Oh, *sir. Please*,
sir."

"And who may you be, *mon enfant*?" inquired
Poirot genially.

"Annie Bates, sir, please sir. I come here to help
Mrs. Ross. I didn't mean, sir, I didn't mean to—to
do anything what I shouldn't do. I did mean it well,
sir. For your good, I mean."

Enlightenment came to Poirot. He held out the
dirty piece of paper.

"Did you write that, Annie?"

"I didn't mean any harm, sir. Really I didn't."

"Of course you didn't, Annie." He smiled at her.
"But tell me about it. Why did you write this?"

"Well, it was them two, sir. Mr. Lee-Wortley and
his sister. Not that she *was* his sister, I'm sure. None
of us thought so! And she wasn't ill a bit. We could
all tell *that*. We thought—we all thought—something
queer was going on. I'll tell you straight, sir. I was in
her bathroom taking in the clean towels, and I lis-

tened at the door. *He* was in her room and they were talking together. I heard what they said plain as plain. 'This detective,' he was saying. 'This fellow Poirot who's coming here. We've got to do something about it. We've got to get him out of the way as soon as possible.' And then he says to her in a nasty, sinister sort of way, lowering his voice, 'Where did you put it?' And she answered him, *'In the pudding.'* Oh, sir, my heart gave such a leap I thought it would stop beating. I thought they meant to poison you in the Christmas pudding. I didn't know *what* to do! Mrs. Ross, she wouldn't listen to the likes of me. Then the idea came to me as I'd write you a warning. And I did and I put it on your pillow where you'd find it when you went to bed." Annie paused breathlessly.

Poirot surveyed her gravely for some minutes.

"You see too many sensational films, I think, Annie," he said at last, "or perhaps it is the television that affects you? But the important thing is that you have the good heart and a certain amount of ingenuity. When I return to London I will send you a present."

"Oh thank you, sir. Thank you very much, sir."

"What would you like, Annie, as a present?"

"Anything I like, sir? Could I have anything I like?"

"Within reason," said Hercule Poirot prudently, "yes."

"Oh sir, could I have a vanity box? A real posh slap up vanity box like the one Mr. Lee-Wortley's sister, wot wasn't his sister, had?"

"Yes," said Poirot, "yes, I think that could be managed.

"It is interesting," he mused. "I was in a museum the other day observing some antiquities from Babylon or one of those places, thousands of years old—and among them were cosmetics boxes. The heart of woman does not change."

"Beg your pardon, sir?" said Annie.

"It is nothing," said Poirot, "I reflect. You shall have your vanity box, child."

"Oh, thank you, sir. Oh, thank you very much indeed, sir."

Annie departed ecstatically. Poirot looked after her, nodding his head in satisfaction.

"Ah," he said to himself. "And now—I go. There is nothing more to be done here."

A pair of arms slipped round his shoulders unexpectedly.

"If you *will* stand just under the mistletoe . . ." said Bridget.

Hercule Poirot enjoyed it. He enjoyed it very much. He said to himself that he had had a very good Christmas.

The Dressmaker's Doll

The doll lay in the big velvet-covered chair. There was not much light in the room; the London skies were dark. In the gentle, greyish-green gloom, the sage-green coverings and the curtains and the rugs all blended with each other. The doll blended, too. She lay long and limp and sprawled in her green-velvet clothes and her velvet cap and the painted mask of her face. She was not a doll as children understand dolls. She was the Puppet Doll, the whim of Rich Women, the doll who lolls beside the telephone, or among the cushions of the divan. She sprawled there, eternally limp and yet strangely alive. She looked a decadent product of the twentieth century.

Sybil Fox, hurrying in with some patterns and a sketch, looked at the doll with a faint feeling of surprise and bewilderment. She wondered—but whatever she wondered did not get to the front of her mind. Instead, she thought to herself, "Now, what's happened to the pattern of the blue velvet? Wherever

93

have I put it? I'm sure I had it here just now." She went out on the landing and called up to the workroom.

"Elspeth. Elspeth, have you the blue pattern up there? Mrs. Fellows-Brown will be here any minute now."

She went in again, switching on the lights. Again she glanced at the doll. "Now where on earth—ah, there it is." She picked the pattern up from where it had fallen from her hand. There was the usual creak outside on the landing as the elevator came to a halt and in a minute or two Mrs. Fellows-Brown, accompanied by her Pekinese, came puffing into the room rather like a fussy local train arriving at a wayside station.

"It's going to pour," she said, "simply *pour!*"

She threw off gloves and a fur. Alicia Coombe came in. She didn't always come in nowadays, only when special customers arrived, and Mrs. Fellows-Brown was such a customer.

Elspeth, the forewoman of the workroom, came down with the frock and Sybil pulled it over Mrs. Fellows-Brown's head.

"There," she said. "It really does suit you. It's a lovely color, isn't it?"

Alicia Coombe sat back a little in her chair, studying it.

"Yes," she said, "I think it's good. Yes, it's definitely a success."

Mrs. Fellows-Brown turned sideways and looked in the mirror.

"I must say," she said, "your clothes do *do* something to my behind."

"You're much thinner than you were three months ago," Sybil assured her.

"I'm really not," said Mrs. Fellows-Brown, "though I must say I *look* it in this. There's something about the way you cut, it really does minimize my behind. I almost look as though I hadn't got one—I mean only the usual kind that most people have." She sighed and gingerly smoothed the troublesome portion of her anatomy. "It's always been a bit of a trial to me," she said. "Of course, for years I could pull it in, you know, by sticking out my front. Well, I can't do that any longer because I've got a stomach now as well as a behind. And I mean—well, you can't pull it in both ways, can you?"

Alicia Coombe said, "You should see some of my customers!"

Mrs. Fellows-Brown experimented to and fro.

"A stomach is worse than a behind," she said. "It shows more. Or perhaps you think it does, because, I mean, when you're talking to people you're facing them and that's the moment they can't see your behind but they can notice your stomach. Anyway, I've made it a rule to pull in my stomach and let my behind look after itself." She craned her neck round still farther, then said suddenly, "Oh, that doll of yours! She gives me the creeps. How long have you had her?"

Sybil glanced uncertainly at Alicia Coombe who looked puzzled but vaguely distressed.

"I don't know exactly . . . some time I think—I never *can* remember things. It's awful nowadays—I simply *cannot* remember. Sybil, how long have we had her?"

Sybil said shortly, "I don't know."

"Well," said Mrs. Fellows-Brown, "she gives *me* the creeps. Uncanny! She looks, you know, as though she was watching us all, and perhaps laughing in that velvet sleeve of hers. I'd get rid of her if I were you.'' She gave a little shiver. Then she plunged once more into dressmaking details. Should she or should she not have the sleeves an inch shorter? And what about the length? When all these important points were settled satisfactorily, Mrs. Fellows-Brown resumed her own garments and prepared to leave. As she passed the doll, she turned her head again.

''No,'' she said, ''I *don't* like that doll. She looks too much as though she *belonged* here. It isn't healthy.''

''Now what did she mean by that?'' demanded Sybil, as Mrs. Fellows-Brown departed down the stairs.

Before Alicia Coombe could answer, Mrs. Fellows-Brown returned, poking her head round the door.

''Good gracious, I forgot all about Fou-Ling. Where are you, ducksie? Well I never!''

She stared and the other two women stared, too. The Pekinese was sitting by the green-velvet chair, staring up at the limp doll sprawled on it. There was no expression, either of pleasure or resentment, on his small popeyed face. He was merely looking.

''Come along, mum's darling,'' said Mrs. Fellows-Brown.

Mum's darling paid no attention whatever.

''He gets more disobedient every day,'' said Mrs. Fellows-Brown, with the air of one cataloguing a virtue. ''Come *on*, Fou-Ling. Dindins. Luffly liver.''

Fou-Ling turned his head about an inch and a half toward his mistress, then with disdain resumed his appraisal of the doll.

"She certainly made an impression on him," said Mrs. Fellows-Brown. "I don't think he's ever noticed her before. *I* haven't either. Was she here last time I came?"

The two other women looked at each other. Sybil now had a frown on her face, and Alicia Coombe said, wrinkling up her forehead, "I told you—I simply can't remember anything nowadays. How long *have* we had her, Sybil?"

"Where did she come from?" demanded Mrs. Fellows-Brown. "Did you buy her?"

"Oh, no." Somehow Alicia Coombe was shocked at the idea. "Oh *no*. I suppose—I suppose someone gave her to me." She shook her head. "Maddening!" she exclaimed. "Absolutely maddening, when everything goes out of your head the very moment after it's happened."

"Now don't be stupid, Fou-Ling," said Mrs. Fellows-Brown sharply. "Come on. I'll have to pick you up."

She picked him up. Fou-Ling uttered a short bark of agonized protest. They went out of the room with Fou-Ling's popeyed face turned over his fluffy shoulder, still staring with enormous attention at the doll on the chair . . .

"That there doll," said Mrs. Groves, "fair gives me the creeps, it does."

Mrs. Groves was the cleaner. She had just finished a crablike progress backward along the floor. Now she was standing up and working slowly round the room with a duster.

"Funny thing," said Mrs. Groves, "never noticed it really until yesterday. And then it hit me all of a sudden, as you might say."

"You don't like it?" asked Sybil.

"I tell you, Mrs. Fox, it gives me the creeps," said the cleaning woman. "It ain't natural, if you know what I mean. All those long hanging legs and the way she's slouched down there and the cunning look she has in her eye. It doesn't look healthy, that's what I say."

"You've never said anything about her before," said Sybil.

"I tell you, I never noticed her—not till this morning . . . Of course I know she's been here some time but—" She stopped and a puzzled expression flitted across her face. "Sort of thing you might dream of at night," she said, and gathering up various cleaning implements she departed from the fitting room and walked across the landing to the room on the other side.

Sybil stared at the relaxed doll. An expression of bewilderment was growing on her face. Alicia Coombe entered and Sybil turned sharply.

"Miss Coombe, how long *have* you had this creature?"

"What, the doll? My dear, you know I can't remember things. Yesterday—why, it's too silly! I was going out to that lecture and I hadn't gone halfway down the street when I suddenly found I couldn't remember where I was going. I thought and I thought. Finally I told myself it *must* be Fortnums. I knew there was something I wanted to get at Fortnums. Well, you won't believe me, it wasn't till I actually got home and was having some tea that I remembered about the lecture. Of course, I've always heard that people go gaga as they get on in life, but it's happening to me much too fast. I've forgotten now where I've put my handbag—and my spectacles, too. Where did I put those spectacles? I had them just now—I was reading something in the *Times*."

"The spectacles are on the mantelpiece here," said Sybil, handing them to her. "How did you get the doll? Who gave her to you?"

"That's a blank, too," said Alicia Coombe. "*Somebody* gave her to me or sent her to me, I suppose . . . However she does seem to match the room very well, doesn't she?"

"Rather too well, I think," said Sybil. "Funny thing is, *I* can't remember when I first noticed her here."

"Now don't you get the same way as I am," Alicia Coombe admonished her. "After all, you're young still."

"But really, Miss Coombe, I don't remember. I mean I looked at her yesterday and thought there was something—well, Mrs. Groves is quite right—something creepy about her. And then I thought I'd already thought so, and then I tried to remember when I first thought so and—well, I just couldn't remember anything! In a way, it was as if I'd never seen her before—only it didn't feel like that. It felt as though she'd been here a long time but I'd only just noticed her."

"Perhaps she flew in through the window one day on a broomstick," said Alicia Coombe. "Anyway, she belongs here now all right." She looked round. "You could hardly imagine the room without her, could you?"

"No," said Sybil, with a slight shiver, "but I rather wish I could."

"Could what?"

"Imagine the room without her."

"Are we all going barmy about this doll?" demanded Alicia Coombe impatiently. "What's wrong with the poor thing? Looks like a decayed cabbage to me, but perhaps," she added, "that's because I haven't got my spectacles on." She put them on her nose and looked firmly at the doll. "Yes," she said, "I see what you mean. She *is* a little creepy . . . Sad-looking but—well, sly and rather determined, too."

"Funny," said Sybil, "Mrs. Fellows-Brown taking such a violent dislike to her."

"She's one who never minds speaking her mind," said Alicia Coombe.

"But it's odd," persisted Sybil, "that this doll should make such an impression on her."

"Well, people do take dislikes very suddenly sometimes."

"Perhaps," said Sybil, with a little laugh, "that doll never *was* here until yesterday . . . Perhaps she just—flew in through the window as you say and settled herself here."

"No," said Alicia Coombe, "I'm sure she's been here some time. Perhaps she only became visible yesterday."

"That's what I feel, too," said Sybil, "that she's been here some time . . . but all the same I *don't* remember really seeing her till yesterday."

"Now, dear," said Alicia Coombe briskly, "do stop it. You're making me feel quite peculiar with shivers running up and down my spine. You're not going to work up a great deal of supernatural hoo-hah about that creature, are you?" She picked up the doll, shook it out, rearranged its shoulders, and sat it down again on another chair. Immediately the doll flopped slightly and relaxed.

"It's not a bit lifelike," said Alicia Coombe, staring at the doll. "And yet, in a funny way, she does seem alive, doesn't she?"

"Oo, it did give me a turn," said Mrs. Groves, as she went round the showroom, dusting. "Such a turn as I hardly like to go into the fitting room any more."

"What's given you a turn?" demanded Miss Coombe, who was sitting at a writing table in the corner, busy with various accounts. "This woman," she added more for her own benefit than that of Mrs. Groves, "thinks she can have two evening dresses, three cocktail dresses, and a suit every year without ever paying me a penny for them! Really, some people!"

"It's that doll," said Mrs. Groves.

"What, our doll again?"

"Yes, sitting up there at the desk, like a human. Oo, it didn't half give me a turn!"

"What are you talking about?"

Alicia Coombe got up, strode across the room, across the little landing outside, and into the room opposite—the fitting room. There was a small Sheraton desk in one corner of it, and there, sitting in a chair drawn up to it, her long floppy arms on the desk, sat the doll.

"Somebody seems to have been having fun," said Alicia Coombe. "Fancy sitting her up like that. Really, she looks quite natural."

Sybil Fox came down the stairs at this moment carrying a dress that was to be tried on that morning.

"Come here, Sybil. Look at our doll sitting at my private desk and writing letters now."

The two women looked.

"Really," said Alicia Coombe, "it's too ridiculous! I wonder who propped her up there. Did you?"

"No, I didn't," said Sybil. "It must have been one of the girls from upstairs."

"A silly sort of joke, really," said Alicia Coombe. She picked up the doll from the desk and threw her back on the sofa.

Sybil laid the dress over a chair carefully, then she went out and up the stairs to the workroom.

"You know the doll," she said, "the velvet doll in Miss Coombe's room downstairs—in the fitting room?"

The forewoman and three of the girls looked up.

"Yes, miss, of course we know."

"Who sat her up at the desk this morning for a joke?"

The three girls looked at her, then Elspeth, the forewoman, said, "Sat her up at the desk? *I* didn't."

"Nor did I," said one of the girls. "Did you, Marlene?" Marlene shook her head.

"This your bit of fun, Elspeth?"

"No, indeed," said Elspeth, a stern woman who looked as though her mouth should always be full of pins. "I've more to do than going about playing with dolls and sitting them up at desks."

"Look here," said Sybil, and to her surprise her voice shook slightly. "It was—it was quite a good joke, only I'd just like to know who did it."

The three girls bristled.

"We've told you, Mrs. Fox. None of us did it, did we, Marlene?"

"I didn't," said Marlene, "and if Nellie and Margaret say they didn't, well then none of us did."

"You've heard what *I* had to say," said Elspeth.

"What's this all about anyway, Mrs. Fox?"

Sybil said slowly, "It just seemed so odd."

"Perhaps it was Mrs. Groves?" said Elspeth.

Sybil shook her head. "It wouldn't be Mrs. Groves. It gave *her* quite a turn."

"I'll come down and see for myself," said Elspeth.

"She's not there now," said Sybil. "Miss Coombe took her away from the desk and threw her back on the sofa. Well—" she paused, "what I mean is, someone must have stuck her up there in the chair at the writing desk—thinking it was funny, I suppose. And—and I don't see why they won't say so."

"I've told you twice, Mrs. Fox," said Margaret. "I don't see why you should go on accusing us of telling lies. None of us would do a silly thing like that."

"I'm sorry," said Sybil, "I didn't mean to upset you. But—but who else could possibly have done it?"

"Perhaps she got up and walked there herself," said Marlene, and giggled.

For some reason Sybil didn't like the suggestion.

"Oh, it's all a lot of nonsense, anyway," she said, and went down the stairs again.

Alicia Coombe was humming quite cheerfully. She looked round the room.

"I've lost my spectacles again," she said, "but it doesn't really matter. I don't want to see anything this moment. The trouble is, of course, when you're as blind as I am, that when you have lost your spectacles, unless you've got another pair to put on and find them with, well then you can't find them because you can't see to find them."

"I'll look round for you," said Sybil. "You had them just now."

"I went into the other room when you went upstairs. I expect I took them back in there."

She went across to the other room.

"It's such a bother," said Alicia Coombe. "I want to get on with these accounts. How can I if I haven't my spectacles?"

"I'll go up and get your second pair from the bedroom," said Sybil.

"I haven't got a second pair at present," said Alicia Coombe.

"Why, what's happened to them?"

"Well, I think I left them yesterday when I was out at lunch. I've rung up there, and I've rung up the two shops I went into, too."

"Oh, dear," said Sybil, "you'll have to get *three* pairs, I suppose."

"If I had three pairs of spectacles," said Alicia Coombe, "I should spend my whole life looking for one or the other of them. I really think it's best to have only *one*. Then you've *got* to look till you find it."

"Well, they must be somewhere," said Sybil. "You haven't been out of these two rooms. They're certainly not here, so you must have laid them down in the fitting room."

She went back, walking round, looking quite closely. Finally, as a last idea, she took up the doll from the sofa.

"I've got them," she called.

"Oh, where were they, Sybil?"

"Under our precious doll. I suppose you must have thrown them down when you put her back on the sofa."

"I didn't. I'm sure I didn't."

"Oh," said Sybil with exasperation. "Then I suppose the doll took them and was hiding them from you!"

"Really, you know," said Alicia, looking thoughtfully at the doll, "I wouldn't put it past her. She looks very intelligent, don't you think, Sybil?"

"I don't think I like her face," said Sybil. "She looks as though she knew something that we didn't."

"You don't think she looks sort of sad and sweet?" said Alicia Coombe, pleadingly, but without conviction.

"I don't think she's in the least sweet," said Sybil.

"No . . . perhaps you're right. . . . Oh, well, let's get on with things. Lady Lee will be here in another ten minutes. I just want to get these invoices done and posted."

"Mrs. Fox. Mrs. Fox."

"Yes, Margaret?" said Sybil. "What is it?"

Sybil was busy leaning over a table, cutting a piece of satin material.

"Oh, Mrs. Fox, it's that doll again. I took down the brown dress like you said, and there's that doll sitting up at the desk again. And it wasn't me—it wasn't any of us. Please, Mrs. Fox, we really wouldn't do such a thing."

Sybil's scissors slid a little.

"There," she said angrily, "look what you've made me do. Oh, well, it'll be all right, I suppose. Now, what's this about the doll?"

"She's sitting at the desk again."

Sybil went down and walked into the fitting room. The doll was sitting at the desk exactly as she had sat there before.

"You're very determined, aren't you?" said Sybil, speaking to the doll.

She picked her up unceremoniously and put her back on the sofa.

"That's your place, my girl," she said. "You stay there."

She walked across to the other room.

"Miss Coombe."

"Yes, Sybil?"

"Somebody *is* having a game with us, you know. That doll was sitting at the desk again."

"Who do you think it is?"

"It must be one of those three upstairs," said Sybil. "Thinks it's funny, I suppose. Of course they all swear to high heaven it wasn't them."

"Who do you think it is—Margaret?"

"No, I don't think it's Margaret. She looked quite queer when she came in and told me. I expect it's that giggling Marlene."

"Anyway, it's a very silly thing to do."

"Of course it is—idiotic," said Sybil. "However," she added grimly, "I'm going to put a stop to it."

"What are you going to do?"

"You'll see," said Sybil.

That night when she left, she locked the fitting-room door from the outside.

"I'm locking this door," she said, "and I'm taking the key with me."

"Oh, I see," said Alicia Coombe, with a faint air of amusement. "You're beginning to think it's me, are you? You think I'm so absent-minded that I go in there and think I'll write at the desk, but instead I pick the doll up and put her there to write for me. Is that the idea? And then I forget all about it?"

"Well, it's a possibility," Sybil admitted. "Anyway, I'm going to be quite sure that no silly practical joke is played tonight."

The following morning, her lips set grimly, the first thing Sybil did on arrival was to unlock the door of the fitting room and march in. Mrs. Groves, with an aggrieved expression and mop and duster in hand, had been waiting on the landing.

"*Now* we'll see!" said Sybil.

Then she drew back with a slight gasp.

The doll was sitting at the desk.

"Coo!" said Mrs. Groves behind her. "It's uncanny! That's what it is. Oh, there, Mrs. Fox, you look quite pale, as though you've come over queer. You need a little drop of something. Has Miss Coombe got a drop upstairs, do you know?"

"I'm quite all right," said Sybil.

She walked over to the doll, lifted her carefully, and crossed the room with her.

"Somebody's been playing a trick on you again," said Mrs. Groves.

"I don't see how they could have played a trick on me this time," said Sybil slowly. "I locked that door last night. You know yourself that no one could get in."

"Somebody's got another key, maybe," said Mrs. Groves, helpfully.

"I don't think so," said Sybil. "We've never bothered to lock this door before. It's one of those old-fashioned keys and there's only one of them."

"Perhaps the other key fits it—the one to the door opposite."

In due course they tried all the keys in the shop, but none fitted the door of the fitting room.

"It *is* odd, Miss Coombe," said Sybil later, as they were having lunch together.

Alicia Coombe was looking rather pleased.

"My dear," she said. "I think it's simply extraordinary. I think we ought to write to the psychical research people about it. You know they might send an investigator—a medium or someone—to see if there's anything peculiar about the room."

"You don't seem to mind at all," said Sybil.

"Well, I rather enjoy it in a way," said Alicia Coombe. "I mean, at my age, it's rather fun when things happen! All the same—no," she added thoughtfully, "I don't think I do quite like it. I mean, that doll's getting rather above herself, isn't she?"

On that evening Sybil and Alicia Coombe locked the door once more on the outside.

"I still think," said Sybil, "that somebody might be playing a practical joke, though really, I don't see why . . ."

"Do you think she'll be at the desk again tomorrow morning?" demanded Alicia.

"Yes," said Sybil, "I do."

But they were wrong. The doll was not at the desk. Instead, she was on the window sill, looking out into the street. And again there was an extraordinary naturalness about her position.

"It's all frightfully silly, isn't it?" said Alicia Coombe, as they were snatching a quick cup of tea that afternoon. By common consent they were not having it in the fitting room, as they usually did, but in Alicia Coombe's own room opposite.

"Silly in what way?"

"Well, I mean, there's nothing you can get hold of. Just a doll that's always in a different place."

As day followed day it seemed a more and more apt observation. It was not only at night that the doll now moved. At any moment when they came into the fitting room, after they had been absent even a few minutes, they might find the doll in a different place. They could have left her on the sofa and find her on a chair. Then she'd be on a different chair. Sometimes she'd be in the window seat, sometimes at the desk again.

"She just moves about as she likes," said Alicia Coombe. "And I think, Sybil, I *think* it's amusing her."

The two women stood looking down at the inert sprawling figure in its limp, soft velvet, with its painted silk face.

"Some old bits of velvet and silk and a lick of paint, that's all it is," said Alicia Coombe. Her voice was strained. "I suppose, you know, we could—er—we could dispose of her."

"What do you mean, dispose of her?" asked Sybil. Her voice sounded almost shocked.

"Well," said Alicia Coombe, "we could put her in the fire, if there was a fire. Burn her, I mean, like a witch . . . Or of course," she added matter-of-factly, "we could just put her in the dustbin."

"I don't think that would do," said Sybil. "Somebody would probably take her out of the dustbin and bring her back to us."

"Or we could send her somewhere," said Alicia Coombe. "You know, to one of those societies who are always writing and asking for something—for a sale or a bazaar. I think that's the best idea."

"I don't know . . ." said Sybil. "I'd be almost afraid to do that."

"Afraid?"

"Well, I think she'd come back," said Sybil.

"You mean, she'd come back *here*?"

"Yes."

"Like a homing pigeon?"

"Yes, that's what I mean."

"I suppose we're not going off our heads, are we?" said Alicia Coombe. "Perhaps I've really gone gaga and perhaps you're just humoring me, is that it?"

"No," said Sybil. "But I've got a nasty frightened feeling—a horrid feeling that she's too strong for us."

"What? That mess of rags?"

"Yes, that horrible limp mess of rags. Because, you see, she's so determined."

"Determined?"

"To have her own way? You mean, this is *her* room now!"

"Yes," said Alicia Coombe, looking round, "it is, isn't it? Of course, it always was, when you come to think of it—the colors and everything . . . I thought she fitted in here, but it's the room that fits her. I must say," added the dressmaker, with a touch of briskness in her voice, "it's rather absurd when a doll comes and takes possession of things like this. You know, Mrs. Groves won't come in here any longer and clean."

"Does she say she's frightened of the doll?"

"No. She just makes excuses of some kind or other." Then Alicia added with a hint of panic, "What are we going to do, Sybil? It's getting me down, you know. I haven't been able to design anything for weeks."

"I can't keep my mind on cutting out properly," Sybil confessed. "I make all sorts of silly mistakes.

Perhaps," she said uncertainly, "your idea of writing to the psychical research people might do some good."

"Just make us look like a couple of fools," said Alicia Coombe. "I didn't seriously mean it. No, I suppose we'll just have to go on until—"

"Until what?"

"Oh, I don't know," said Alicia, and she laughed uncertainly.

On the following day Sybil, when she arrived, found the door of the fitting room locked.

"Miss Coombe, have you got the key? Did you lock this last night?"

"Yes," said Alicia Coombe, "I locked it and it's going to stay locked."

"What do you mean?"

"I just mean I've given up the room. The doll can have it. We don't need two rooms. We can fit in here."

"But it's your own private sitting room."

"Well, I don't want it any more. I've got a very nice bedroom. I can make a bed-sitting room out of that, can't I?"

"Do you mean you're really not going into that fitting room ever again?" said Sybil incredulously.

"That's exactly what I mean."

"But—what about cleaning? It'll get in a terrible state."

"Let it!" said Alicia Coombe. "If this place is suffering from some kind of possession by a doll, all right—let her keep possession. And clean the room herself." And she added, "She hates us, you know."

"What do you mean?" said Sybil. "The doll *hates* us?"

"Yes," said Alicia. "Didn't you know? You must

have known. You must have seen it when you looked at her.''

''Yes,'' said Sybil thoughtfully, ''I suppose I did. I suppose I felt like that all along—that she hated us and wanted to get us out of there.''

''She's a malicious little thing,'' said Alicia Coombe. ''Anyway, she ought to be satisfied now.''

Things went on rather more peacefully after that. Alicia Coombe announced to her staff that she was giving up the use of the fitting room for the present—it made too many rooms to dust and clean, she explained.

But it hardly helped her to overhear one of the work girls saying to another on the evening of the same day, ''She really is batty, Miss Coombe is now. I always thought she was a bit queer—the way she lost things and forgot things. But it's really beyond anything now, isn't it? She's got a sort of thing about that doll downstairs.''

''Ooo, you don't think she'll go really bats, do you?'' said the other girl. ''That she might knife us or something?''

They passed, chattering, and Alicia sat up indignantly in her chair. Going bats indeed! Then she added ruefully, to herself, ''I suppose, if it wasn't for Sybil, I should think myself that I was going bats. But with me and Sybil and Mrs. Groves too, well, it does look as though there was *something* in it. But what I don't see is, how is it going to end?''

Three weeks later, Sybil said to Alicia Coombe, ''We've got to go into that room *sometime*.''

''Why?''

''Well, I mean, it must be in a filthy state. Moths

will be getting into things, and all that. We ought just to dust and sweep it and then lock it up again.''

"I'd much rather keep it shut up and not go back in there," said Alicia Coombe.

Sybil said, "Really, you know, you're even more superstitious than I am."

"I suppose I am," said Alicia Coombe. "I was much more ready to believe in all this than you were, but to begin with, you know—I—well, I found it exciting in an odd sort of way. I don't know. I'm just scared, and I'd rather not go into that room again."

"Well, I want to," said Sybil, "and I'm going to."

"You know what's the matter with you?" said Alicia Coombe. "You're simply curious, that's all."

"All right, then I'm curious. I want to see what the doll's done."

"I still think it's much better to leave her alone," said Alicia. "Now we've got out of that room, she's satisfied. You'd better leave her satisfied." She gave an exasperated sigh. "What nonsense we are talking!"

"Yes, I know we're talking nonsense, but if you tell me of any way of *not* talking nonsense—come on, now, give me that key."

"All right, all right."

"I believe you're afraid I'll let her out or something. I should think she was the kind that could pass through doors or windows."

Sybil unlocked the door and went in.

"How terribly odd," she said.

"What's odd?" said Alicia Coombe, peering over her shoulder.

"The room hardly seems dusty at all, does it? You'd think, after being shut up all this time—"

"Yes, it is odd."

"There she is," said Sybil.

The doll was on the sofa. She was not lying in her usual limp position. She was sitting upright, a cushion behind her back. She had the air of the mistress of the house, waiting to receive people.

"Well," said Alicia Coombe, "she seems at home all right, doesn't she? I almost feel I ought to apologize for coming in."

"Let's go," said Sybil.

She backed out, pulled the door to, and locked it again.

The two women gazed at each other.

"I wish I knew," said Alicia Coombe, "why it scares us so much . . ."

"My goodness, who wouldn't be scared?"

"Well, I mean, what *happens*, after all? It's nothing really—just a kind of puppet that gets moved around the room. I expect it isn't the puppet itself— it's a poltergeist."

"Now that *is* a good idea."

"Yes, but I don't really believe it. I think it's—it's that doll."

"Are you *sure* you don't know where she really came from?"

"I haven't the faintest idea," said Alicia. "And the more I think of it the more I'm perfectly certain that I didn't buy her, and that nobody gave her to me. I think she—well, she just came."

"Do you think she'll—ever go?"

"Really," said Alicia, "I don't see why she should . . . She's got all she wants."

But it seemed that the doll had not got all she wanted. The next day, when Sybil went into the showroom, she drew in her breath with a sudden gasp. Then she called up the stairs.

"Miss Coombe, Miss Coombe, come down here."

"What's the matter?"

Alicia Coombe, who had got up late, came down the stairs, hobbling a little precariously for she had rheumatism in her right knee.

"What is the matter with you, Sybil?"

"Look. Look what's happened now."

They stood in the doorway of the showroom. Sitting on a sofa, sprawled easily over the arm of it, was the doll.

"She's got out," said Sybil. "*She's got out of that room!* She wants this room as well."

Alicia Coombe sat down by the door. "In the end," she said, "I suppose she'll want the whole shop."

"She might," said Sybil.

"You nasty, sly, malicious brute," said Alicia, addressing the doll. "What do you want to come and pester us so? We don't want you."

It seemed to her, and to Sybil too, that the doll moved very slightly. It was as though its limbs relaxed still further. A long limp arm was lying on the arm of the sofa and the half-hidden face looked as if it were peering from under the arm. And it was a sly, malicious look.

"Horrible creature," said Alicia. "I can't bear it! I can't bear it any longer."

Suddenly, taking Sybil completely by surprise, she dashed across the room, picked up the doll, ran to the window, opened it, and flung the doll out into the street. There was a gasp and a half cry of fear from Sybil.

"Oh, Alicia, you shouldn't have done that! I'm sure you shouldn't have done that!"

"I had to do something," said Alicia Coombe. "I just couldn't stand it any more."

Sybil joined her at the window. Down below on the pavement the doll lay, loose-limbed, face down.

"You've *killed* her," said Sybil.

"Don't be absurd . . . How can I kill something that's made of velvet and silk, bits and pieces. It's not real."

"It's horribly real," said Sybil.

Alicia caught her breath.

"Good heavens. That child—"

A small ragged girl was standing over the doll on the pavement. She looked up and down the street—a street that was not unduly crowded at this time of the morning though there was some automobile traffic; then, as though satisfied, the child bent, picked up the doll, and ran across the street.

"Stop, stop!" called Alicia.

She turned to Sybil.

"That child mustn't take the doll. She *mustn't*! That doll is dangerous—it's evil. We've got to stop her."

It was not they who stopped her. It was the traffic. At that moment three taxis came down one way and two tradesmen's vans in the other direction. The child was marooned on an island in the middle of the road. Sybil rushed down the stairs, Alicia Coombe following her. Dodging between a tradesman's van and a private car, Sybil, with Alicia Coombe directly behind her, arrived on the island before the child could get through the traffic on the opposite side.

"You can't take that doll," said Alicia Coombe. "Give her back to me."

The child looked at her. She was a skinny little girl about eight years old, with a slight squint. Her face was defiant.

"Why should I give 'er to you?" she said. "Pitched her out of the window, you did—I saw you. If you pushed her out of the window you don't want her, so now she's mine."

"I'll buy you another doll," said Alicia frantically. "We'll go to a toy shop—anywhere you like—and I'll buy you the best doll we can find. But give me back this one."

"Shan't," said the child.

Her arms went protectingly round the velvet doll.

"You *must* give her back," said Sybil. "She isn't yours."

She stretched out to take the doll from the child and at that moment the child stamped her foot, turned, and screamed at them.

"Shan't! Shan't! Shan't! She's my very own. I love her. *You* don't love her. You hate her. If you didn't hate her you wouldn't of pushed her out of the window. I love her, I tell you, and that's what she wants. She *wants* to be loved."

And then like an eel, sliding through the vehicles, the child ran across the street, down an alleyway, and out of sight before the two older women could decide to dodge the cars and follow.

"She's gone," said Alicia.

"She said the doll wanted to be loved," said Sybil.

"Perhaps," said Alicia, "perhaps that's what she wanted all along . . . to be loved . . ."

In the middle of the London traffic the two frightened women stared at each other.

Greenshaw's Folly

The two men rounded the corner of the shrubbery.

"Well, there you are," said Raymond West. "That's it."

Horace Bindler took a deep, appreciative breath.

"But my dear," he cried, "how wonderful." His voice rose in a high screech of esthetic delight, then deepened in reverent awe. "It's unbelievable. Out of this world! A period piece of the best."

"I thought you'd like it," said Raymond West, complacently.

"Like it? My dear—" Words failed Horace. He unbuckled the strap of his camera and got busy. "This will be one of the gems of my collection," he said happily. "I do think, don't you, that it's rather amusing to have a collection of monstrosities? The idea came to me one night seven years ago in my bath. My last real gem was in the Campo Santo at Genoa, but I really think this beats it. What's it called?"

"I haven't the least idea," said Raymond.

"I suppose it's got a name?"

"It must have. But the fact is that it's never re-
ferred to round here as anything but Greenshaw's
Folly."

"Greenshaw being the man who built it?"

"Yes. In 1860 or '70 or thereabouts. The local success story of the time. Barefoot boy who had risen to
immense prosperity. Local opinion is divided as to
why he built this house, whether it was sheer exuberance of wealth or whether it was done to impress
his creditors. If the latter, it didn't impress them. He
either went bankrupt or the next thing to it. Hence
the name, Greenshaw's Folly."

Horace's camera clicked. "There," he said in a
satisfied voice. "Remind me to show you Number
310 in my collection. A really incredible marble mantelpiece in the Italian manner." He added, looking at
the house, "I can't conceive of how Mr. Greenshaw
thought of it all."

"Rather obvious in some ways," said Raymond.
"He had visited the *châteaux* of the Loire, don't you
think? Those turrets. And then, rather unfortunately, he seems to have traveled in the Orient. The
influence of the Taj Mahal is unmistakable. I rather
like the Moorish wing," he added, "and the traces of
a Venetian palace."

"One wonders how he ever got hold of an architect
to carry out these ideas."

Raymond shrugged his shoulders.

"No difficulty about that, I expect," he said.
"Probably the architect retired with a good income
for life while poor old Greenshaw went bankrupt."

"Could we look at it from the other side?" asked Horace, "or are we trespassing?"

"We're trespassing all right," said Raymond, "but I don't think it will matter."

He turned toward the corner of the house and Horace skipped after him.

"But who lives here, my dear? Orphans or holiday visitors? It can't be a school. No playing fields or brisk efficiency."

"Oh, a Greenshaw lives here still," said Raymond over his shoulder. "The house itself didn't go in the crash. Old Greenshaw's son inherited it. He was a bit of a miser and lived here in a corner of it. Never spent a penny. Probably never had a penny to spend. His daughter lives here now. Old lady—very eccentric."

As he spoke Raymond was congratulating himself on having thought of Greenshaw's Folly as a means of entertaining his guest. These literary critics always professed themselves as longing for a weekend in the country, and were wont to find the country extremely boring when they got there. Tomorrow there would be the Sunday papers, and for today Raymond West congratulated himself on suggesting a visit to Greenshaw's Folly to enrich Horace Bindler's well-known collection of monstrosities.

They turned the corner of the house and came out on a neglected lawn. In one corner of it was a large artificial rockery, and bending over it was a figure at the sight of which Horace clutched Raymond delightedly by the arm.

"My dear," he exclaimed, "do you see what she's got on? A sprigged print dress. Just like a housemaid—when there were housemaids. One of my most cherished memories is staying at a house in the country when I was quite a boy where a real housemaid called you in the morning, all crackling in a print dress and a cap. Yes, my boy, *really*—a cap. Muslin with streamers. No, perhaps it was the parlormaid who had the streamers. But anyway she was a real housemaid and she brought in an enormous brass can of hot water. What an exciting day we're having."

The figure in the print dress had straightened up and turned toward them, trowel in hand. She was a sufficiently startling figure. Unkempt locks of iron-grey fell wispily on her shoulders and a straw hat, rather like the hats that horses wear in Italy, was crammed down on her head. The colored print dress she wore fell nearly to her ankles. Out of a weather-beaten, not too clean face, shrewd eyes surveyed them appraisingly.

"I must apologize for trespassing, Miss Greenshaw," said Raymond West, as he advanced toward her, "but Mr. Horace Bindler who is staying with me—"

Horace bowed and removed his hat.

"—is most interested in—er—ancient history and —er—fine buildings."

Raymond West spoke with the ease of a famous author who knows that he is a celebrity, that he can venture where other people may not.

Miss Greenshaw looked up at the sprawling exuberance behind her.

"It *is* a fine house," she said appreciatively. "My grandfather built it—before my time, of course. He is reported as having said that he wished to astonish the natives."

"I'll say he did that, ma'am," said Horace Bindler.

"Mr. Bindler is the well-known literary critic," said Raymond West.

Miss Greenshaw had clearly no reverence for literary critics. She remained unimpressed.

"I consider it," said Miss Greenshaw, referring to the house, "as a monument to my grandfather's genius. Silly fools come here and ask me why I don't sell it and go and live in a flat. What would *I* do in a flat? It's my home and I live in it," said Miss Greenshaw. "Always have lived here." She considered, brooding over the past. "There were three of us. Laura married the curate. Papa wouldn't give her any money, said clergymen ought to be unworldly. She died, having a baby. Baby died, too. Nettie ran away with the riding master. Papa cut her out of his will, of course. Handsome fellow, Harry Fletcher, but no good. Don't think Nettie was happy with him. Anyway, she didn't live long. They had a son. He writes to me sometimes, but of course he isn't a Greenshaw. *I*'m the last of the Greenshaws." She drew up her bent shoulders with a certain pride, and readjusted the rakish angle of the straw hat. Then, turning, she said sharply:

"Yes, Mrs. Cresswell, what is it?"

Approaching them from the house was a figure that, seen side by side with Miss Greenshaw, seemed ludicrously dissimilar. Mrs. Cresswell had a marvelously dressed head of well-blued hair towering upward in meticulously arranged curls and rolls. It was as though she had dressed her head to go as a French marquise to a fancy dress party. The rest of her middle-aged person was dressed in what ought to have been rustling black silk but was actually one of the shinier varieties of black rayon. Although she was not a large woman, she had a well-developed and sumptuous bosom. Her voice, when she spoke, was unexpectedly deep. She spoke with exquisite diction —only a slight hesitation over words beginning with "h" and the final pronunciation of them with an exaggerated aspirate gave rise to a suspicion that at some remote period in her youth she might have had trouble over dropping her h's.

"The fish, madam," said Mrs. Cresswell, "the slice of cod. It has not arrived. I have asked Alfred to go down for it and he refuses."

Rather unexpectedly, Miss Greenshaw gave a cackle of laughter.

"Refuses, does he?"

"Alfred, madam, has been most disobliging."

Miss Greenshaw raised two earth-stained fingers to her lips, suddenly produced an ear-splitting whistle and at the same time yelled, "Alfred. Alfred, come here."

Round the corner of the house a young man appeared in answer to the summons, carrying a spade in his hand. He had a bold, handsome face and as he drew near he cast an unmistakably malevolent glance toward Mrs. Cresswell.

"You wanted me, miss?" he said.

"Yes, Alfred. I hear you've refused to go down for the fish. What about it, eh?"

Alfred spoke in a surly voice.

"I'll go down for it if you wants it, miss. You've only got to say."

"I do want it. I want it for my supper."

"Right you are, miss. I'll go right away."

He threw an insolent glance at Mrs. Cresswell, who flushed and murmured below her breath.

"Now that I think of it," said Miss Greenshaw, "a couple of strange visitors are just what we need, aren't they, Mrs. Cresswell?"

Mrs. Cresswell looked puzzled.

"I'm sorry, madam—"

"For you-know-what," said Miss Greenshaw, nodding her head. "Beneficiary to a will mustn't witness it. That's right, isn't it?" She appealed to Raymond West.

"Quite correct," said Raymond.

"I know enough law to know that," said Miss Greenshaw, "and you two are men of standing."

She flung down the trowel on her weeding basket.

"Would you mind coming up to the library with me?"

"Delighted," said Horace eagerly.

She led the way through French windows and through a vast yellow and gold drawing-room with faded brocade on the walls and dust covers arranged over the furniture, then through a large dim hall, up a staircase, and into a room on the second floor.

"My grandfather's library," she announced.

Horace looked round with acute pleasure. It was a room from his point of view quite full of monstrosities. The heads of sphinxes appeared on the most unlikely pieces of furniture, there was a colossal bronze representing, he thought, Paul and Virginia, and a vast bronze clock with classical motifs of which he longed to take a photograph.

"A fine lot of books," said Miss Greenshaw.

Raymond was already looking at the books. From

what he could see from a cursory glance there was no book here of any real interest or, indeed, any book which appeared to have been read. They were all superbly bound sets of the classics as supplied ninety years ago for furnishing a gentleman's library. Some novels of a bygone period were included. But they too showed little signs of having been read.

Miss Greenshaw was fumbling in the drawers of a vast desk. Finally she pulled out a parchment document.

"My will," she explained. "Got to leave your money to someone—or so they say. If I died without a will, I suppose that son of a horse coper would get it. Handsome fellow, Harry Fletcher, but a rogue if ever there was one. Don't see why *his* son should inherit this place. No," she went on, as though answering some unspoken objection, "I've made up my mind. I'm leaving it to Cresswell."

"Your housekeeper?"

"Yes. I've explained it to her. I make a will leaving her all I've got and then I don't need to pay her any wages. Saves me a lot in current expenses, and it keeps her up to the mark. No giving me notice and walking off at any minute. Very la-di-dah and all that, isn't she? But her father was a working plumber in a very small way. *She's* nothing to give herself airs about."

By now Miss Greenshaw had unfolded the parchment. Picking up a pen, she dipped it in the inkstand and wrote her signature, *Katherine Dorothy Greenshaw*.

"That's right," she said. "You've seen me sign it, and then you two sign it, and that makes it legal."

She handed the pen to Raymond West. He hesi-

tated a moment, feeling an unexpected repulsion to
what he was asked to do. Then he quickly scrawled
his well-known autograph, for which his morning's
mail usually brought at least six requests.

Horace took the pen from him and added his own
minute signature.

"That's done," said Miss Greenshaw.

She moved across to the bookcases and stood looking at them uncertainly, then she opened a glass
door, took out a book, and slipped the folded parchment inside.

"I've my own places for keeping things," she said.

"*Lady Audley's Secret*," Raymond West remarked, catching sight of the title as she replaced the
book.

Miss Greenshaw gave another cackle of laughter.

"Best-seller in its day," she remarked. "But not
like your books, eh?"

She gave Raymond a sudden friendly nudge in the
ribs. Raymond was rather surprised that she even
knew he wrote books. Although Raymond West was
a "big name" in literature, he could hardly be described as a best-seller. Though softening a little with
the advent of middle-age, his books dealt bleakly
with the sordid side of life.

"I wonder," Horace demanded breathlessly, "if I
might just take a photograph of the clock."

"By all means," said Miss Greenshaw. "It came, I
believe, from the Paris Exhibition."

"Very probably," said Horace. He took his picture.

"This room's not been used much since my grandfather's time," said Miss Greenshaw. "This desk's
full of old diaries of his. Interesting, I should think. I

haven't the eyesight to read them myself. I'd like to get them published, but I suppose one would have to work on them a good deal.''

"You could engage someone to do that," said Raymond West.

"Could I really? It's an idea, you know. I'll think about it."

Raymond West glanced at his watch.

"We mustn't trespass on your kindness any longer," he said.

"Pleased to have seen you," said Miss Greenshaw graciously. "Thought you were the policeman when I heard you coming round the corner of the house."

"Why a policeman?" demanded Horace, who never minded asking questions.

Miss Greenshaw responded unexpectedly.

"If you want to know the time, ask a policeman," she carolled, and with this example of Victorian wit she nudged Horace in the ribs and roared with laughter.

"It's been a wonderful afternoon," sighed Horace as they walked home. "Really, that place has *everything*. The only thing the library needs is a body. Those old-fashioned detective stories about murder in the library—that's just the kind of library I'm sure the authors had in mind."

"If you want to discuss murder," said Raymond, "you must talk to my Aunt Jane."

"Your Aunt Jane? Do you mean Miss Marple?" Horace felt a little at a loss.

The charming old-world lady to whom he had been introduced the night before seemed the last person to be mentioned in connection with murder.

"Oh, yes," said Raymond. "Murder is a specialty of hers."

"But my dear, how intriguing! What do you really mean?"

"I mean just that," said Raymond. He paraphrased: "Some commit murder, some get mixed up in murders, others have murder thrust upon them. My Aunt Jane comes into the third category."

"You are joking."

"Not in the least. I can refer you to the former Commissioner of Scotland Yard, several Chief Constables, and one or two hard-working inspectors of the C.I.D."

Horace said happily that wonders would never cease. Over the tea table they gave Joan West, Raymond's wife, Louise Oxley, her niece, and old Miss Marple, a résumé of the afternoon's happenings, recounting in detail everything that Miss Greenshaw had said to them.

"But I do think," said Horace, "that there is something a little *sinister* about the whole setup. That duchess-like creature, the housekeeper—arsenic, perhaps, in the teapot, now that she knows her mistress has made the will in her favor?"

"Tell us, Aunt Jane," said Raymond. "Will there be murder or won't there? What do *you* think?"

"I think," said Miss Marple, winding up her wool with a rather severe air, "that you shouldn't joke about these things as much as you do, Raymond. Arsenic is, of course, *quite* a possibility. So easy to obtain. Probably present in the tool shed already in the form of weed killer."

"Oh, really, darling," said Joan West, affectionately. "Wouldn't that be rather too obvious?"

"It's all very well to make a will," said Raymond.
"I don't suppose the poor old thing has anything to
leave except that awful white elephant of a house,
and who would want that?"

"A film company possibly," said Horace, "or a
hotel or an institution?"

"They'd expect to buy it for a song," said Raymond, but Miss Marple was shaking her head.

"You know, dear Raymond, I cannot agree with
you there. About the money, I mean. The grandfather was evidently one of those lavish spenders who
make money easily but can't keep it. He may have
gone broke, as you say, but hardly bankrupt or else
his son would not have had the house. Now the son,
as is so often the case, was of an entirely different
character from his father. A miser. A man who saved
every penny. I should say that in the course of his
lifetime he probably put by a very good sum. This
Miss Greenshaw appears to have taken after him—to
dislike spending money, that is. Yes, I should think it
quite likely that she has quite a substantial sum
tucked away."

"In that case," said Joan West, "I wonder now—
what about Louise?"

They looked at Louise as she sat, silent, by the fire.

Louise was Joan West's niece. Her marriage had
recently, as she herself put it, come unstuck, leaving
her with two young children and a bare sufficiency of
money to keep them on.

"I mean," said Joan, "if this Miss Greenshaw
really wants someone to go through diaries and get a
book ready for publication . . ."

"It's an idea," said Raymond.

Louise said in a low voice, "It's work I could do—and I think I'd enjoy it."

"I'll write to her," said Raymond.

"I wonder," said Miss Marple thoughtfully, "what the old lady meant by that remark about a policeman?"

"Oh, it was just a joke."

"It reminded me," said Miss Marple, nodding her head vigorously, "yes, it reminded me very much of Mr. Naysmith."

"Who was Mr. Naysmith?" asked Raymond, curiously.

"He kept bees," said Miss Marple, "and was very good at doing the acrostics in the Sunday papers. And he liked giving people false impressions just for fun. But sometimes it led to trouble."

Everybody was silent for a moment, considering Mr. Naysmith, but as there did not seem to be any points of resemblance between him and Miss Greenshaw, they decided that dear Aunt Jane was perhaps getting a *little* bit disconnected in her old age.

Horace Bindler went back to London without having collected any more monstrosities and Raymond West wrote a letter to Miss Greenshaw telling her that he knew of a Mrs. Louise Oxley who would be competent to undertake work on the diaries. After a lapse of some days a letter arrived, written in spidery old-fashioned handwriting, in which Miss Greenshaw declared herself anxious to avail herself of the services of Mrs. Oxley, and making an appointment for Mrs. Oxley to come and see her.

Louise duly kept the appointment, generous terms were arranged, and she started work the following day.

"I'm awfully grateful to you," she said to Raymond. "It will fit in beautifully. I can take the children to school, go on to Greenshaw's Folly, and pick them up on my way back. How fantastic the whole setup is! That old woman has to be seen to be believed."

On the evening of her first day at work she returned and described her day.

"I've hardly seen the housekeeper," she said. "She came in with coffee and biscuits at half-past eleven with her mouth pursed up very prunes and prisms, and would hardly speak to me. I think she disapproves deeply of my having been engaged." She went on, "It seems there's quite a feud between her and the gardener, Alfred. He's a local boy and fairly lazy, I should imagine, and he and the housekeeper won't speak to each other. Miss Greenshaw said in her rather grand way, 'There have always been feuds as far as I can remember between the garden and the house staff. It was so in my grandfather's time. There were three men and a boy in the garden then, and eight maids in the house, but there was always friction.' "

On the next day Louise returned with another piece of news.

"Just fancy," she said, "I was asked to ring up the nephew today."

"Miss Greenshaw's nephew?"

"Yes. It seems he's an actor playing in the stock company that's doing a summer season at Boreham-on-Sea. I rang up the theater and left a message asking him to lunch tomorrow. Rather fun, really. The old girl didn't want the housekeeper to know. I think Mrs. Cresswell has done something that's annoyed her."

"Tomorrow another installment of this thrilling serial," murmured Raymond.

"It's exactly like a serial, isn't it? Reconciliation with the nephew, blood is thicker than water— another will to be made and the old will destroyed.

"Aunt Jane, you're looking very serious."

"Was I, my dear? Have you heard any more about the policeman?"

Louise looked bewildered. "I don't know anything about a policeman."

"That remark of hers, my dear," said Miss Marple, "must have meant something."

Louise arrived at her work the following day in a cheerful mood. She passed through the open front door—the doors and windows of the house were always open. Miss Greenshaw appeared to have no fear of burglars, and was probably justified, as most things in the house weighed several tons and were of no marketable value.

Louise had passed Alfred in the drive. When she first noticed him he had been leaning against a tree smoking a cigarette, but as soon as he had caught sight of her he had seized a broom and begun diligently to sweep leaves. An idle young man, she thought, but good-looking. His features reminded her of someone. As she passed through the hall on her way upstairs to the library, she glanced at the large picture of Nathaniel Greenshaw which presided over the mantelpiece, showing him in the acme of Victorian prosperity, leaning back in a large armchair, his hands resting on the gold Albert across his capacious stomach. As her glance swept up from the stomach to the face with its heavy jowls, its bushy eyebrows and its flourishing black mustache, the thought occurred to her that Nathaniel Greenshaw must have been handsome as a young man. He had looked, perhaps, a little like Alfred . . .

She went into the library on the second floor, shut the door behind her, opened her typewriter, and got out the diaries from the drawer at the side of her desk. Through the open window she caught a glimpse of Miss Greenshaw below, in a puce-colored sprigged print, bending over the rockery, weeding assiduously. They had had two wet days, of which the weeds had taken full advantage.

Louise, a town-bred girl, decided that if she ever had a garden it would never contain a rockery which needed weeding by hand. Then she settled down to her work.

When Mrs. Cresswell entered the library with the coffee tray at half-past eleven, she was clearly in a very bad temper. She banged the tray down on the table and observed to the universe:

"Company for lunch—and nothing in the house! What am *I* supposed to do, I should like to know? And no sign of Alfred."

"He was sweeping in the drive when I got here," Louise offered.

"I daresay. A nice soft job."

Mrs. Cresswell swept out of the room, slamming the door behind her. Louise grinned to herself. She wondered what "the nephew" would be like.

She finished her coffee and settled down to her work again. It was so absorbing that time passed quickly. Nathaniel Greenshaw, when he started to keep a diary, had succumbed to the pleasures of frankness. Typing out a passage relating to the personal charms of a barmaid in the neighboring town, Louise reflected that a good deal of editing would be necessary.

As she was thinking this, she was startled by a scream from the garden. Jumping up, she ran to the open window. Below her Miss Greenshaw was staggering away from the rockery toward the house. Her hands were clasped to her breast and between her hands there protruded a feathered shaft that Louise recognized with stupefaction to be the shaft of an arrow.

Miss Greenshaw's head, in its battered straw hat, fell forward on her breast. She called up to Louise in a failing voice: ". . . shot . . . he shot me . . . with an arrow . . . get help . . ."

Louise rushed to the door. She turned the handle, but the door would not open. It took her a moment or two of futile endeavor to realize that she was locked in. She ran back to the window and called down.

"I'm locked in!"

Miss Greenshaw, her back toward Louise and swaying a little on her feet, was calling up to the housekeeper at a window farther along.

"Ring police . . . telephone . . ."

Then, lurching from side to side like a drunkard, Miss Greenshaw disappeared from Louise's view through the window and staggered into the drawing-room on the ground floor. A moment later Louise heard a crash of broken china, a heavy fall, and then silence. Her imagination reconstructed the scene.

Miss Greenshaw must have stumbled blindly into a small table with a Sèvres tea set on it.

Desperately Louise pounded on the library door, calling and shouting. There was no creeper or drainpipe outside the window that could help her to get out that way.

Tired at last of beating on the door, Louise returned to the window. From the window of her sitting-room farther along, the housekeeper's head appeared.

"Come and let me out, Mrs. Oxley. I'm locked in."

"So am I."

"Oh, dear, isn't it awful? I've telephoned the police. There's an extension in this room, but what I can't understand, Mrs. Oxley, is our being locked in. *I* never heard a key turn, did you?"

"No. I didn't hear anything at all. Oh, dear, what shall we do? Perhaps Alfred might hear us." Louise shouted at the top of her voice, "Alfred, Alfred."

"Gone to his dinner as likely as not. What time is it?"

Louise glanced at her watch.

"Twenty-five past twelve."

"He's not supposed to go until half-past, but he sneaks off earlier whenever he can."

"Do you think—do you think—"

Louise meant to ask "Do you think she's dead?" —but the words stuck in her throat.

There was nothing to do but wait. She sat down on the window sill. It seemed an eternity before the stolid helmeted figure of a police constable came round the corner of the house. She leaned out of the window and he looked up at her, shading his eyes with his hand.

"What's going on here?" he demanded.

From their respective windows, Louise and Mrs. Cresswell poured a flood of excited information down on him.

The constable produced a notebook and a pencil. "You ladies ran upstairs and locked yourselves in? Can I have your names, please?"

"Somebody locked us in. Come and let us out."

The constable said reprovingly, "All in good time," and disappeared through the French window below.

Once again time seemed infinite. Louise heard the sound of a car arriving, and, after what seemed an hour, but was actually only three minutes, first Mrs. Cresswell and then Louise were released by a police sergeant more alert than the original constable.

"Miss Greenshaw?" Louise's voice faltered. "What—what's happened?"

The sergeant cleared his throat.

"I'm sorry to have to tell you, madam," he said, "what I've already told Mrs. Cresswell here. Miss Greenshaw is dead."

"Murdered," said Mrs. Cresswell. "That's what it is—murder."

The sergeant said dubiously, "Could have been an accident—some country lads shooting arrows."

Again there was the sound of a car arriving.

The sergeant said, "That'll be the M.O." and he started downstairs.

But it was not the M.O. As Louise and Mrs. Cresswell came down the stairs, a young man stepped hesitatingly through the front door and paused, looking round him with a somewhat bewildered air.

Then, speaking in a pleasant voice that in some way seemed familiar to Louise—perhaps it reminded her of Miss Greenshaw's—he asked, "Excuse me, does—er—does Miss Greenshaw live here?"

"May I have your name if you please," said the sergeant, advancing upon him.

"Fletcher," said the young man. "Nat Fletcher. I'm Miss Greenshaw's nephew, as a matter of fact."

"Indeed, sir, well—I'm sorry—"

"Has anything happened?" asked Nat Fletcher.

"There's been an—accident. Your aunt was shot with an arrow—penetrated the jugular vein—"

Mrs. Cresswell spoke hysterically and without her usual refinement: "Your h'aunt's been murdered, that's what's 'appened. Your h'aunt's been murdered."

Inspector Welch drew his chair a little nearer to the table and let his gaze wander from one to the other of the four people in the room. It was evening of the same day. He had called at the Wests' house to take Louise Oxley once more over her statement.

"You are sure of the exact words? *Shot—he shot me—with an arrow—get help?*"

Louise nodded.

"And the time?"

"I looked at my watch a minute or two later—it was then 12:25—"

"Your watch keeps good time?"

"I looked at the clock as well." Louise left no doubt of her accuracy.

The Inspector turned to Raymond West.

"It appears, sir, that about a week ago you and a Mr. Horace Bindler were witnesses to Miss Greenshaw's will?"

Briefly, Raymond recounted the events of the afternoon visit he and Horace Bindler had paid to Greenshaw's Folly.

"This testimony of yours may be important," said Welch. "Miss Greenshaw distinctly told you, did she, that her will was being made in favor of Mrs. Cresswell, the housekeeper, and that she was not paying Mrs. Cresswell any wages in view of the expectations Mrs. Cresswell had of profiting by her death?"

"That is what she told me—yes."

"Would you say that Mrs. Cresswell was definitely aware of these facts?"

"I should say undoubtedly. Miss Greenshaw made a reference in my presence to beneficiaries not being able to witness a will and Mrs. Cresswell clearly understood what she meant by it. Moreover, Miss Greenshaw herself told me that she had come to this arrangement with Mrs. Cresswell."

"So Mrs. Cresswell had reason to believe she was an interested party. Motive clear enough in her case, and I daresay she'd be our chief suspect now if it wasn't for the fact that she was securely locked in her room like Mrs. Oxley here, and also that Miss Greenshaw definitely said a *man* shot her—"

"She definitely *was* locked in her room?"

"Oh, yes. Sergeant Cayley let her out. It's a big old-fashioned lock with a big old-fashioned key. The key was in the lock and there's not a chance that it could have been turned from inside or any hanky-panky of that kind. No, you can *take* it definitely that Mrs. Cresswell was locked inside that room and couldn't get out. And there were no bows and arrows in the room and Miss Greenshaw couldn't in any case have been shot from her window—the angle forbids it. No, Mrs. Cresswell's out.''

He paused, then went on: "Would you say that Miss Greenshaw, in your opinion, was a practical joker?''

Miss Marple looked up sharply from her corner.

"So the will wasn't in Mrs. Cresswell's favor after all?'' she said.

Inspector Welch looked over at her in a rather surprised fashion.

"That's a very clever guess of yours, madam,'' he said. "No. Mrs. Cresswell isn't named as beneficiary.''

"Just like Mr. Naysmith,'' said Miss Marple, nodding her head. "Miss Greenshaw told Mrs. Cresswell she was going to leave her everything and so got out of paying her wages; and then she left her money to somebody else. No doubt she was vastly pleased with herself. No wonder she chortled when she put the will away in *Lady Audley's Secret*.''

"It was lucky Mrs. Oxley was able to tell us about the will and where it was put,'' said the Inspector. "We might have had a long hunt for it otherwise.''

"A Victorian sense of humor,'' murmured Raymond West.

"So she left her money to her nephew after all,'' said Louise.

The Inspector shook his head.

"No,'' he said, "she didn't leave it to Nat Fletcher. The story goes around here—of course I'm new to the place and I only get the gossip that's second-hand —but it seems that in the old days both Miss Green-

shaw and her sister were set on the handsome young
riding master, and the sister got him. No, she didn't
leave the money to her nephew—'' Inspector Welch
paused, rubbing his chin. ''She left it to Alfred,'' he
said.

''Alfred—the gardener?'' Joan spoke in a surprised voice.

''Yes, Mrs. West. Alfred Pollock.''

''But why?'' cried Louise.

Miss Marple coughed and murmured, ''I would
imagine, though perhaps I am wrong, that there may
have been—what we might call *family* reasons.''

''You could call them that in a way,'' agreed the
Inspector. ''It's quite well-known in the village, it
seems, that Thomas Pollock, Alfred's grandfather,
was one of old Mr. Greenshaw's bye-blows.''

''Of course,'' cried Louise, ''the resemblance!''

She remembered how after passing Alfred she had
come into the house and looked up at old Greenshaw's portrait.

''I daresay,'' said Miss Marple, ''that she thought
Alfred Pollock might have a pride in the house,
might even want to live in it, whereas her nephew
would almost certainly have no use for it whatever
and would sell it as soon as he could possibly do so.
He's an actor, isn't he? What play exactly is he acting
in at present?''

Trust an old lady to wander from the point,
thought Inspector Welch; but he replied civilly, ''I
believe, madam, they are doing a season of Sir James
M. Barrie's plays.''

''Barrie,'' said Miss Marple thoughtfully.

''*What Every Woman Knows*,'' said Inspector
Welch, and then blushed. ''Name of a play,'' he said

quickly. "I'm not much of a theater-goer myself," he added, "but the wife went along and saw it last week. Quite well done, she said it was."

"Barrie wrote some very charming plays," said Miss Marple, "though I must say that when I went with an old friend of mine, General Easterly, to see Barrie's *Little Mary*—" she shook her head sadly "—neither of us knew where to look."

The Inspector, unacquainted with the play *Little Mary*, seemed completely fogged.

Miss Marple explained: "When I was a girl, Inspector, nobody ever mentioned the word *stomach*."

The Inspector looked even more at sea. Miss Marple was murmuring titles under her breath.

"*The Admirable Crichton*. Very clever. *Mary Rose*—a charming play. I cried, I remember. *Quality Street* I didn't care for so much. Then there was *A Kiss for Cinderella*. Oh, of course!"

Inspector Welch had no time to waste on theatrical discussion. He returned to the matter at hand.

"The question is," he said, "did Alfred Pollock know the old lady had made a will in his favor? Did she tell him?" He added, "You see—there's an Archery Club over at Boreham—and *Alfred Pollock's a member*. He's a very good shot indeed with a bow and arrow."

"Then isn't your case quite clear?" asked Raymond West. "It would fit in with the doors being locked on the two women—he'd know just where they were in the house."

The Inspector looked at him. He spoke with deep melancholy.

"He's got an alibi," said the Inspector.

"I always think alibis are definitely suspicious," Raymond remarked.

"Maybe, sir," said Inspector Welch. "You're talking as a writer."

"I don't write detective stories," said Raymond West, horrified at the mere idea.

"Easy enough to say that alibis are suspicious," went on Inspector Welch, "but unfortunately we've got to deal with facts." He sighed. "We've got three good suspects," he went on. "Three people who, as it happened, were very close upon the scene at the time. Yet the odd thing is that it looks as though none of the three could have done it. The housekeeper I've already dealt with; the nephew, Nat Fletcher, at the moment Miss Greenshaw was shot, was a couple of miles away filling up his car at a garage and asking his way; as for Alfred Pollock, six people will swear that he entered the Dog and Duck at twenty past twelve and was there for an hour having his usual bread and cheese and beer."

"Deliberately establishing an alibi," said Raymond West hopefully.

"Maybe," said Inspector Welch, "but if so, he *did* establish it."

There was a long silence. Then Raymond turned his head to where Miss Marple sat upright and thoughtful.

"It's up to you, Aunt Jane," he said. "The Inspector's baffled, the Sergeant's baffled, I'm baffled, Joan's baffled, Louise is baffled. But to you, Aunt Jane, it is crystal clear. Am I right?"

"I wouldn't say that," said Miss Marple, "not *crystal* clear. And murder, dear Raymond, isn't a game. I don't suppose poor Miss Greenshaw wanted to die, and it was a particularly brutal murder. Very well-planned and quite cold-blooded. It's not a thing to make *jokes* about."

"I'm sorry," said Raymond. "I'm not really as callous as I sound. One treats a thing lightly to take away from the—well, the horror of it."

"That is, I believe, the modern tendency," said Miss Marple. "All these wars, and having to joke about funerals. Yes, perhaps I was thoughtless when I implied that you were callous."

"It isn't," said Joan, "as though we'd known her at all well."

"That is *very* true," said Miss Marple. "You, dear Joan, did not know her at all. I did not know her at all. Raymond gathered an impression of her from one afternoon's conversation. Louise knew her for only two days."

"Come now, Aunt Jane," said Raymond, "tell us your views. You don't mind, Inspector?"

"Not at all," said the Inspector politely.

"Well, my dear, it would seem that we have three people who had—or might have thought they had—a motive to kill the old lady. And three quite simple reasons why none of the three could have done so. The housekeeper could not have killed Miss Greenshaw because she was locked in her room and because her mistress definitely stated that a *man* shot her. The gardener was inside the Dog and Duck at the time, the nephew at the garage."

"Very clearly put, madam," said the Inspector.

"And since it seems most unlikely that any outsider should have done it, where, then, are we?"

"That's what the Inspector wants to know," said Raymond West.

"One so often looks at a thing the wrong way round," said Miss Marple apologetically. "If we can't alter the movements or the positions of those three people, then couldn't we perhaps alter the time of the murder?"

"You mean that both my watch and the clock were wrong?" asked Louise.

"No, dear," said Miss Marple, "I didn't mean that at all. I mean that the murder didn't occur when you thought it occurred."

"But I *saw* it," cried Louise.

"Well, what I have been wondering, my dear, was whether you weren't *meant* to see it. I've been asking myself, you know, whether that wasn't the real reason why you were engaged for this job."

"What *do* you mean, Aunt Jane?"

"Well, dear, it seems odd. Miss Greenshaw did not like spending money—yet she engaged you and agreed quite willingly to the terms you asked. It seems to me that perhaps you were meant to be there in that library on the second floor, looking out of the window so that you could be the key witness—someone from outside of irreproachably good character—to fix a definite time and place for the murder."

"But you can't mean," said Louise, incredulously, "that Miss Greenshaw *intended* to be murdered."

"What I mean, dear," said Miss Marple, "is that you didn't really know Miss Greenshaw. There's no real reason, is there, why the Miss Greenshaw you saw when you went up to the house should be the same Miss Greenshaw that Raymond saw a few days earlier? Oh, yes, I know,'' she went on, to prevent Louise's reply, ''she was wearing the peculiar old-fashioned print dress and the strange straw hat, and had unkempt hair. She corresponded exactly to the description Raymond gave us last weekend. But those two women, you know, were much the same age, height, and size. The housekeeper, I mean, and Miss Greenshaw.''

''But the housekeeper is fat!'' Louise exclaimed. ''She's got an enormous bosom.''

Miss Marple coughed.

''But my dear, surely, nowadays I have seen—er—them myself in shops most indelicately displayed. It is very easy for anyone to have a—a bosom—of *any* size and dimension.''

''What are you trying to say?'' demanded Raymond.

''I was just thinking that during the two days Louise was working there, one woman could have played both parts. You said yourself, Louise, that you hardly saw the housekeeper, except for the one minute in the morning when she brought you the tray with coffee. One sees those clever artists on the stage coming in as different characters with only a moment or two to spare, and I am sure the change could have been effected quite easily. That marquise headdress could be just a wig slipped on and off.''

''Aunt Jane! Do you mean that Miss Greenshaw was dead before I started work there?''

''Not dead. Kept under drugs, I should say. A very easy job for an unscrupulous woman like the housekeeper to do. Then she made the arrangements with you and got you to telephone to the nephew to ask him to lunch at a definite time. The only person who would have known that this Miss Greenshaw was *not* Miss Greenshaw would have been Alfred. And if you remember, the first two days you were working there it was wet, and Miss Greenshaw stayed in the house. Alfred never came into the house because of his feud with the housekeeper. And on the last morning Alfred was in the drive, while Miss Greenshaw was working on the rockery—I'd like to have a look at that rockery."

"Do you mean it was Mrs. Cresswell who killed Miss Greenshaw?"

"I think that after bringing you your coffee, the housekeeper locked the door on you as she went out, then carried the unconscious Miss Greenshaw down to the drawing-room, then assumed her 'Miss Greenshaw' disguise and went out to work on the rockery where you could see her from the upstairs window. In due course she screamed and came staggering to the house clutching an arrow as though it had penetrated her throat. She called for help and was careful to say '*he* shot me' so as to remove suspicion from the housekeeper—from herself. She also called up to the housekeeper's window as though she saw her there. Then, once inside the drawing-room, she threw over a table with porcelain on it, ran quickly upstairs, put on her marquise wig, and was able a few moments later to lean her head out of the window and tell you that she, too, was locked in."

"But she *was* locked in," said Louise.

"I know. That is where the policeman comes in."

"What policeman?"

"Exactly—what policeman? I wonder, Inspector, if you would mind telling me how and when *you* arrived on the scene?"

The Inspector looked a little puzzled.

"At 12:29 we received a telephone call from Mrs. Cresswell, housekeeper to Miss Greenshaw, stating that her mistress had been shot. Sergeant Cayley and myself went out there at once in a car and arrived at the house at 12:35. We found Miss Greenshaw dead and the two ladies locked in their rooms."

"So, you see, my dear," said Miss Marple to Louise. "The police constable *you* saw wasn't a real police constable at all. You never thought of him again—one doesn't—one just accepts one more uniform as part of the Law."

"But who—why?"

"As to who—well, if they are playing *A Kiss for Cinderella*, a policeman is the principal character. Nat Fletcher would only have to help himself to the costume he wears on the stage. He'd ask his way at a garage, being careful to call attention to the time—12:25; then he would drive on quickly, leave his car round a corner, slip on his police uniform, and do his 'act.' "

"But why—why?"

"*Someone* had to lock the housekeeper's door on the outside, and someone had to drive the arrow through Miss Greenshaw's throat. You can stab anyone with an arrow just as well as by shooting it—but it needs force."

"You mean they were both in it?"

"Oh, yes, I think so. Mother and son as likely as not."

"But Miss Greenshaw's sister died long ago."

"Yes, but I've no doubt Mr. Fletcher married again—he sounds like the sort of man who would. I think it possible that the child died too, and that this so-called nephew was the second wife's child, and not really a relation at all. The woman got the post as housekeeper and spied out the land. Then he wrote to Miss Greenshaw as her nephew and proposed to call on her—he may have even made some joking reference to coming in his policeman's uniform—remember, she said she was expecting a policeman. But I think Miss Greenshaw suspected the truth and refused to see him. He would have been her heir if she had died without making a will—but of course once she had made a will in the housekeeper's favor, as they thought, then it was clear sailing."

"But why use an arrow?" objected Joan. "So very far-fetched."

"Not far-fetched at all, dear. Alfred belonged to an Archery Club—Alfred was meant to take the blame. The fact that he was in the pub as early as 12:20 was most unfortunate from their point of view. He always left a little before his proper time and that would have been just right." She shook her head. "It really seems all wrong—morally, I mean, that Alfred's laziness should have saved his life."

The Inspector cleared his throat.

"Well, madam, these suggestions of yours are very interesting. I shall, of course, have to investigate—"

Miss Marple and Raymond West stood by the rockery and looked down at a gardening basket full of dying vegetation.

Miss Marple murmured:

"Alyssum, saxifrage, cystis, thimble campanula . . . Yes, that's all the proof *I* need. Whoever was weeding here yesterday morning was no gardener— she pulled up plants as well as weeds. So now I *know*

I'm right. Thank you, dear Raymond, for bringing me here. I wanted to see the place for myself."

She and Raymond both looked up at the outrageous pile of Greenshaw's Folly.

A cough made them turn. A handsome young man was also looking at the monstrous house.

"Plaguey big place," he said. "Too big for nowadays—or so they say. I dunno about that. If I won a football pool and made a lot of money, that's the kind of house I'd like to build."

He smiled bashfully at them, then rumpled his hair.

"Reckon I can say so now—that there house was built by my great-grandfather," said Alfred Pollock. "And a fine house it is, for all they call it Greenshaw's Folly!"

The Double Clue

"But above everything—no publicity," said Mr. Marcus Hardman for perhaps the fourteenth time.

The word *publicity* occurred throughout his conversation with the regularity of a leitmotif. Mr. Hardman was a small man, delicately plump, with exquisitely manicured hands and a plaintive tenor voice. In his way, he was somewhat of a celebrity and the fashionable life was his profession. He was rich, but not remarkably so, and he spent his money zealously in the pursuit of social pleasure. His hobby was collecting. He had the collector's soul. Old lace, old fans, antique jewelry—nothing crude or modern for Marcus Hardman.

Poirot and I, obeying an urgent summons, had arrived to find the little man writhing in an agony of indecision. Under the circumstances, to call in the police was abhorrent to him. On the other hand, not to call them in was to acquiesce in the loss of some of the gems of his collection. He hit upon Poirot as a compromise.

"My rubies, Monsieur Poirot, and the emerald necklace—said to have belonged to Catherine de Medici. Oh, the emerald necklace!"

"If you will recount to me the circumstances of their disappearance?" suggested Poirot gently.

"I am endeavoring to do so. Yesterday afternoon I had a little tea party—quite an informal affair, some half a dozen people or so. I have given one or two of them during the season, and though perhaps I should not say so, they have been quite a success. Some good music—Nacora, the pianist, and Katherine Bird, the Australian contralto—in the big studio. Well, early in the afternoon, I was showing my guests my collection of medieval jewels. I keep them in the small wall safe over there. It is arranged like a cabinet inside, with colored velvet background, to display the stones. Afterward we inspected the fans—in that case on the wall. Then we all went to the studio for music. It was not until after everyone had gone that I discovered the safe rifled! I must have failed to shut it properly, and someone had seized the opportunity to denude it of its contents. The rubies, Monsieur Poirot, the emerald necklace—the collection of a lifetime! What would I not give to recover them! But there must be no publicity! You fully understand that, do you not, Monsieur Poirot? My own guests, my personal friends! It would be a horrible scandal!"

"Who was the last person to leave this room when you went to the studio?"

"Mr. Johnston. You may know him? The South African millionaire. He has just rented the Abbotburys' house in Park Lane. He lingered behind a few moments, I remember. But surely, oh, surely it could not be he!"

"Did any of your guests return to this room during the afternoon on any pretext?"

"I was prepared for that question, Monsieur Poirot. Three of them did so. Countess Vera Rossakoff, Mr. Bernard Parker, and Lady Runcorn."

"Let us hear about them."

"The Countess Rossakoff is a very charming Russian lady, a member of the old régime. She has recently come to this country. She had bade me goodbye, and I was therefore somewhat surprised to find her in this room apparently gazing in rapture at my cabinet of fans. You know, Monsieur Poirot, the more I think of it, the more suspicious it seems to me. Don't you agree?"

"Extremely suspicious; but let us hear about the others."

"Well, Parker simply came here to fetch a case of miniatures that I was anxious to show to Lady Runcorn."

"And Lady Runcorn herself?"

"As I daresay you know, Lady Runcorn is a middle-aged woman of considerable force of character who devotes most of her time to various charitable committees. She simply returned to fetch a handbag she had laid down somewhere."

"*Bien, monsieur.* So we have four possible suspects. The Russian countess, the English *grand dame*, the South African millionaire, and Mr. Bernard Parker. Who *is* Mr. Parker, by the way?"

The question appeared to embarrass Mr. Hardman considerably.

"He is—er—he is a young fellow. Well, in fact, a young fellow I know."

"I had already deduced as much," replied Poirot

gravely. "What does he do, this Mr. Parker?"

"He is a young man about town—not, perhaps, quite in the swim, if I may so express myself."

"How did he come to be a friend of yours, may I ask?"

"Well—er—on one or two occasions he has—performed certain little commissions for me."

"Continue, monsieur," said Poirot.

Hardman looked piteously at him. Evidently the last thing he wanted to do was to continue. But as Poirot maintained an inexorable silence, he capitulated.

"You see, Monsieur Poirot—it is well known that I am interested in antique jewels. Sometimes there is a family heirloom to be disposed of—which, mind you, would never be sold in the open market or to a dealer. But a private sale to me is a very different matter. Parker arranges the details of such things, he is in touch with both sides, and thus any little embarrassment is avoided. He brings anything of that kind to my notice. For instance, the Countess Rossakoff has brought some family jewels with her from Russia. She is anxious to sell them. Bernard Parker was to have arranged the transaction."

"I see," said Poirot thoughtfully. "And you trust him implicitly?"

"I have had no reason to do otherwise."

"Mr. Hardman, of these four people, which do you yourself suspect?"

"Oh, Monsieur Poirot, what a question! They are my friends, as I told you. I suspect none of them—or all of them, whichever way you like to put it."

"I do not agree. You suspect one of those four. It is not Countess Rossakoff. It is not Mr. Parker. Is it

Lady Runcorn or Mr. Johnston?"

"You drive me into a corner, Monsieur Poirot, you do indeed. I am most anxious to have no scandal. Lady Runcorn belongs to one of the oldest families in England; but it is true, it is most unfortunately true, that her aunt, Lady Caroline, suffered from a most melancholy affliction. It was understood, of course, by all her friends, and her maid returned the teaspoons, or whatever it was, as promptly as possible. You see my predicament!"

"So Lady Runcorn had an aunt who was a kleptomaniac? Very interesting. You permit that I examine the safe?"

Mr. Hardman assenting, Poirot pushed back the door of the safe and examined the interior. The empty velvet-lined shelves gaped at us.

"Even now the door does not shut properly," murmured Poirot, as he swung it to and fro. "I wonder why? Ah, what have we here? A glove, caught in the hinge. A man's glove."

He held it out to Mr. Hardman.

"That's not one of my gloves," the latter declared.

"Aha! Something more!" Poirot bent deftly and picked up a small object from the floor of the safe. It was a flat cigarette case made of black moiré.

"My cigarette case!" cried Mr. Hardman.

"Yours? Surely not, monsieur. Those are not your initials."

He pointed to an entwined monogram of two letters executed in platinum.

Hardman took it in his hand.

"You are right," he declared. "It is very like mine, but the initials are different. A *'P'* and a *'B.'* Good heavens—Parker!"

"It would seem so," said Poirot. "A somewhat careless young man—especially if the glove is his also. That would be a double clue, would it not?"

"Bernard Parker!" murmured Hardman. "What a relief! Well, Monsieur Poirot, I leave it to you to recover the jewels. Place the matter in the hands of the police if you think fit—that is, if you are quite sure that it is he who is guilty."

"See you, my friend," said Poirot to me, as we left the house together, "he has one law for the titled, and another law for the plain, this Mr. Hardman. Me, I have not yet been ennobled, so I am on the side of the plain. I have sympathy for this young man. The whole thing was a little curious, was it not? There was Hardman suspecting Lady Runcorn; there was I, suspecting the Countess and Johnston; and all the time, the obscure Mr. Parker was our man."

"Why did you suspect the other two?"

"*Parbleu!* It is such a simple thing to be a Russian refugee or a South African millionaire. Any woman can call herself a Russian countess; anyone can buy a house in Park Lane and call himself a South African millionaire. Who is going to contradict them? But I observe that we are passing through Bury Street. Our careless young friend lives here. Let us, as you say, strike while the iron is in the fire."

Mr. Bernard Parker was at home. We found him reclining on some cushions, clad in an amazing dressing gown of purple and orange. I have seldom taken a greater dislike to anyone than I did to this particular young man with his white, effeminate face and affected lisping speech.

"Good morning, monsieur," said Poirot briskly.

"I come from Mr. Hardman. Yesterday, at the party, somebody has stolen all his jewels. Permit me to ask you, monsieur—is this your glove?"

Mr. Parker's mental processes did not seem very rapid. He stared at the glove, as though gathering his wits together.

"Where did you find it?" he asked at last.

"Is it your glove, monsieur?"

Mr. Parker appeared to make up his mind.

"No, it isn't," he declared.

"And this cigarette case, is that yours?"

"Certainly not. I always carry a silver one."

"Very well, monsieur. I go to put matters in the hands of the police."

"Oh, I say, I wouldn't do that, if I were you," cried Mr. Parker in some concern. "Beastly unsympathetic people, the police. Wait a bit. I'll go round and see old Hardman. Look here—oh, stop a minute."

But Poirot beat a determined retreat.

"We have given him something to think about, have we not?" he chuckled. "Tomorrow we will observe what has occurred."

But we were destined to have a reminder of the Hardman case that afternoon. Without the least warning the door flew open, and a whirlwind in human form invaded our privacy, bringing with her a swirl of sables (it was as cold as only an English June day can be) and a hat rampant with slaughtered ospreys. Countess Vera Rossakoff was a somewhat disturbing personality.

"You are Monsieur Poirot? What is this that you have done? You accuse that poor boy! It is infamous. It is scandalous. I know him. He is a chicken, a lamb—never would he steal. He has done everything for me. Will I stand by and see him martyred and butchered?''

"Tell me, madame, is this his cigarette case?" Poirot held out the black moiré case.

The Countess paused for a moment while she inspected it.

"Yes, it is his. I know it well. What of it? Did you find it in the room? We were all there; he dropped it then, I suppose. Ah, you policemen, you are worse than the Red Guards—"

"And is this his glove?"

"How should I know? One glove is like another. Do not try to stop me—he must be set free. His character must be cleared. You shall do it. I will sell my jewels and give you much money."

"Madame—"

"It is agreed, then? No, no, do not argue. The poor boy! He came to me, the tears in his eyes. 'I will save you,' I said. 'I will go to this man—this ogre, this monster! Leave it to Vera.' Now it is settled, I go."

With as little ceremony as she had come, she swept from the room, leaving an overpowering perfume of an exotic nature behind her.

"What a woman!" I exclaimed. "And what furs!"

"Ah, yes, *they* were genuine enough! Could a spurious countess have real furs? My little joke, Hastings. . . . No, she is truly Russian, I fancy. Well, well, so Master Bernard went bleating to her."

"The cigarette case is his. I wonder if the glove is also—"

With a smile Poirot drew from his pocket a second glove and placed it by the first. There was no doubt of their being a pair.

"Where did you get the second one, Poirot?"

"It was thrown down with a stick on the table in the hall in Bury Street. Truly, a very careless young man, Monsieur Parker. Well, well, *mon ami*—we must be thorough. Just for the form of the thing, I will make a little visit to Park Lane."

Needless to say, I accompanied my friend. Johnston was out, but we saw his private secretary. It transpired that Johnston had only recently arrived from South Africa. He had never been in England before.

"He is interested in precious stones, is he not?" hazarded Poirot.

"Gold mining is nearer the mark," laughed the secretary.

Poirot came away from the interview thoughtful. Late that evening, to my utter surprise, I found him earnestly studying a Russian grammar.

"Good heavens, Poirot!" I cried. "Are you learning Russian in order to converse with the Countess in her own language?"

"She certainly would not listen to my English, my friend!"

"But surely, Poirot, well-born Russians invariably speak French?"

"You are a mine of information, Hastings! I will cease puzzling over the intricacies of the Russian alphabet."

He threw the book from him with a dramatic gesture. I was not entirely satisfied. There was a twinkle in his eye which I knew of old. It was an invariable sign that Hercule Poirot was pleased with himself.

"Perhaps," I said sapiently, "you doubt her being really a Russian. You are going to test her?"

"Ah, no, no, she is Russian all right."

"Well, then—"

"If you really want to distinguish yourself over this case, Hastings, I recommend 'First Steps in Russian' as an invaluable aid."

Then he laughed and would say no more. I picked up the book from the floor and dipped into it curiously, but could make neither head nor tail of Poirot's remarks.

The following morning brought us no news of any kind, but that did not seem to worry my little friend. At breakfast, he announced his intention of calling upon Mr. Hardman early in the day. We found the elderly society butterfly at home, and seemingly a little calmer than on the previous day.

"Well, Monsieur Poirot, any news?" he demanded eagerly.

Poirot handed him a slip of paper.

"That is the person who took the jewels, monsieur. Shall I put matters in the hands of the police? Or would you prefer me to recover the jewels without bringing the police into the matter?"

Mr. Hardman was staring at the paper. At last he found his voice.

"Most astonishing. I should infinitely prefer to have no scandal in the matter. I give you *carte blanche*, Monsieur Poirot. I am sure you will be discreet."

Our next procedure was to hail a taxi, which Poirot ordered to drive to the Carlton. There he inquired for Countess Rossakoff. In a few minutes we were ushered up into the lady's suite. She came to meet us with outstretched hands, arrayed in a marvelous negligee of barbaric design.

"Monsieur Poirot!" she cried. "You have succeeded? You have cleared that poor infant?"

"Madame la Comtesse, your friend Mr. Parker is perfectly safe from arrest."

"Ah, but you are the clever little man! Superb! And so quickly too."

"On the other hand, I have promised Mr. Hardman that the jewels shall be returned to him today."

"So?"

"Therefore, madame, I should be extremely obliged if you would place them in my hands without delay. I am sorry to hurry you, but I am keeping a taxi—in case it should be necessary for me to go on to Scotland Yard; and we Belgians, madame, we practice the thrift."

The Countess had lighted a cigarette. For some seconds she sat perfectly still, blowing smoke rings, and gazing steadily at Poirot. Then she burst into a laugh, and rose. She went across to the bureau, opened a drawer, and took out a black silk handbag. She tossed it lightly to Poirot. Her tone, when she spoke, was perfectly light and unmoved.

"We Russians, on the contrary, practice prodigality," she said. "And to do that, unfortunately, one must have money. You need not look inside. They are all there."

Poirot arose.

"I congratulate you, madame, on your quick intelligence and your promptitude."

"Ah! But since you were keeping your taxi waiting, what else could I do?"

"You are too amiable, madame. You are remaining long in London?"

"I am afraid not—owing to you."

"Accept my apologies."

"We shall meet again elsewhere, perhaps."

"I hope so."

"And I—do not!" exclaimed the Countess with a laugh. "It is a great compliment that I pay you there—there are very few men in the world whom I fear. Goodbye, Monsieur Poirot."

"Goodbye, Madame la Comtesse. Ah—pardon me, I forgot! Allow me to return you your cigarette case."

And with a bow he handed to her the little black moiré case we had found in the safe. She accepted it without any change of expression—just a lifted eyebrow and a murmured: "I see!"

"What a woman!" cried Poirot enthusiastically as we descended the stairs. "*Mon Dieu, quelle femme!* Not a word of argument—of protestation, of bluff! One quick glance, and she had sized up the position correctly. I tell you, Hastings, a woman who can accept defeat like that—with a careless smile—will go far! She is dangerous; she has the nerves of steel; she—" He tripped heavily.

"If you can manage to moderate your transports and look where you're going, it might be as well," I suggested. "When did you first suspect the Countess?"

"*Mon ami*, it was the glove *and* the cigarette case —the double clue, shall we say?—that worried me. Bernard Parker might easily have dropped one or the other—but hardly both. Ah, no, that would have been *too* careless! In the same way, if someone else had placed them there to incriminate Parker, one would have been sufficient—the cigarette case *or* the glove—again not both. So I was forced to the conclusion that one of the two things did *not* belong to Parker. I imagined at first that the case was his, and that the glove was not. But when I discovered the fellow to the glove, I saw that it was the other way about. Whose, then, was the cigarette case? Clearly, it could not belong to Lady Runcorn. The initials were wrong. Mr. Johnston? Only if he were here under a false name. I interviewed his secretary, and it was apparent at once that everything was clear and aboveboard. There was no reticence about Mr. Johnston's past. The Countess, then? She was supposed to have brought jewels with her from Russia; she had only to take the stones from their settings, and it was extremely doubtful if they could ever be identified. What could be easier for her than to pick up one of Parker's gloves from the hall that day and thrust it into the safe? But, *bien sûr*, she did not intend to drop her own cigarette case."

"But if the case was hers, why did it have '*B. P.*' on it? The Countess' initials are *V. R.*"

Poirot smiled gently upon me.

"Exactly, *mon ami*; but in the Russian alphabet, *B* is *V* and *P* is *R*."

"Well, you couldn't expect me to guess that. I don't know Russian."

"Neither do I, Hastings. That is why I bought my little book—and urged it on your attention."

He sighed.

"A remarkable woman. I have a feeling, my friend—a very decided feeling—I shall meet her again. Where, I wonder?"

The Last Séance

Raoul Daubreuil crossed the Seine humming a little
tune to himself. He was a good-looking young
Frenchman of about thirty-two, with a fresh-colored
face and a little black moustache. By profession he
was an engineer. In due course he reached the Car-
donet and turned in at the door of No. 17. The con-
cierge looked out from her lair and gave him a grudg-
ing "Good-morning," to which he replied cheerfully.
Then he mounted the stairs to the apartment on the
third floor. As he stood there waiting for his ring
at the bell to be answered he hummed once more his
little tune. Raoul Daubreuil was feeling particularly
cheerful this morning. The door was opened by an
elderly Frenchwoman, whose wrinkled face broke
into smiles when she saw who the visitor was.

"Good-morning, monsieur."

"Good-morning, Elise," said Raoul.

He passed into the vestibule, pulling off his gloves
as he did so.

"Madame expects me, does she not?" he asked over his shoulder.

"Ah, yes, indeed, monsieur."

Elise shut the front door and turned towards him.

"If Monsieur will pass into the little salon, Madame will be with him in a few minutes. At the moment she reposes herself."

Raoul looked up sharply. "Is she not well?"

"Well!"

Elise gave a snort. She passed in front of Raoul and opened the door of the little salon for him. He went in and she followed him.

"Well!" she continued. "How should she be well, poor lamb? Séances, séances, and always séances! It is not right—not natural, not what the good God intended for us. For me, I say straight out, it is trafficking with the devil."

Raoul patted her on the shoulder reassuringly.

"There, there, Elise," he said soothingly, "do not excite yourself, and do not be too ready to see the devil in everything you do not understand."

Elise shook her head doubtingly.

"Ah, well," she grumbled under her breath, "Monsieur may say what he pleases, I don't like it. Look at Madame, every day she gets whiter and thinner, and the headaches!"

She held up her hands. "Ah, no, it is not good, all this spirit business. Spirits indeed! All the good spirits are in paradise, and the others are in purgatory."

"Your view of the life after death is refreshingly simple, Elise," said Raoul as he dropped into a chair.

The old woman drew herself up. "I am a good Catholic, monsieur."

She crossed herself, went towards the door, then paused, her hand on the handle.

"Afterwards when you are married, monsieur," she said pleadingly, "it will not continue—all this?"

Raoul smiled at her affectionately.

"You are a good faithful creature, Elise," he said, "and devoted to your mistress. Have no fear, once she is my wife, all this 'spirit business' as you call it, will cease. For Madame Daubreuil there will be no more séances."

Elise's face broke into smiles.

"Is it true what you say?" she asked eagerly.

The other nodded gravely.

"Yes," he said, speaking almost more to himself than to her. "Yes, all this must end. Simone has a wonderful gift and she has used it freely, but now she has done her part. As you have justly observed, Elise, day by day she gets whiter and thinner. The life of a medium is a particularly trying and arduous one, involving a terrible nervous strain. All the same, Elise, your mistress is the most wonderful medium in Paris—more, in France. People from all over the world come to her because they know that with her there is no trickery, no deceit."

Elise gave a snort of contempt.

"Deceit! Ah, no, indeed. Madame could not deceive a new-born babe if she tried."

"She is an angel," said the young Frenchman with fervor. "And I—I shall do everything a man can to make her happy. You believe that?"

Elise drew herself up, and spoke with a certain simple dignity.

"I have served Madame for many years, monsieur. With all respect I may say that I love her. If I did not

believe that you adored her as she deserves to be
adored—*eh bien*, monsieur! I should be willing to
tear you limb from limb.''

Raoul laughed. "Bravo, Elise! You are a faithful
friend, and you must approve of me now that I have
told you Madame is going to give up the spirits.''

He expected the old woman to receive this pleas-
antry with a laugh, but somewhat to his surprise she
remained grave.

"Supposing, monsieur," she said hesitatingly,
"the spirits will not give her up?''

Raoul stared at her. "Eh! What do you mean?''

"I said,'' repeated Elise, "supposing the spirits
will not give her up?''

"I thought you didn't believe in the spirits, Elise?''

"No more I do,'' said Elise stubbornly. "It is
foolish to believe in them. All the same . . .''

"Well?''

"It is difficult for me to explain, monsieur. You
see, me, I always thought that these mediums, as they
call themselves, were just clever cheats who imposed
on the poor souls who had lost their dear ones. But
Madame is not like that. Madame is good. Madame
is honest, and . . .''

She lowered her voice and spoke in a tone of awe.

"Things happen. It is not trickery, things happen,
and that is why I am afraid. For I am sure of this,
monsieur, it is not right. It is against nature and *le
bon Dieu*, and somebody will have to pay.''

Raoul got up from his chair and came and patted
her on the shoulder.

"Calm yourself, my good Elise,'' he said, smiling.
"See, I will give you some good news. Today is the

last of these séances; after today there will be no more."

"There is one today, then?" asked the old woman suspiciously.

"The last, Elise, the last."

Elise shook her head disconsolately. "Madame is not fit . . ." she began.

But her words were interrupted, the door opened and a tall, fair woman came in. She was slender and graceful, with the face of a Botticelli Madonna. Raoul's face lighted up, and Elise withdrew quickly and discreetly.

"Simone!"

He took both her long, white hands in his and kissed each in turn. She murmured his name very softly.

"Raoul, my dear one."

Again he kissed her hands and then looked intently into her face.

"Simone, how pale you are! Elise told me you were resting; you are not ill, my well-beloved?"

"No, not ill . . ." she hesitated.

He led her over to the sofa and sat down on it beside her.

"But tell me then."

The medium smiled faintly. "You will think me foolish," she murmured.

"I? Think you foolish? Never."

Simone withdrew her hand from his grasp. She sat perfectly still for a moment or two gazing down at the carpet. Then she spoke in a low, hurried voice.

"I am afraid, Raoul."

He waited for a minute or two expecting her to go

on, but as she did not he said encouragingly:

"Yes, afraid of what?"

"Just afraid . . . that is all."

"But . . ."

He looked at her in perplexity, and she answered the look quickly.

"Yes, it is absurd, isn't it, and yet I feel just that. Afraid, nothing more. I don't know what of, or why, but all the time I am possessed with the idea that something terrible—terrible, is going to happen to me. . . ."

She stared out in front of her. Raoul put an arm gently round her.

"My dearest," he said, "come, you must not give way. I know what it is, the strain, Simone, the strain of a medium's life. All you need is rest—rest and quiet."

She looked at him gratefully. "Yes, Raoul, you are right. That is what I need, rest and quiet."

She closed her eyes and leant back a little against his arm.

"And happiness," murmured Raoul in her ear.

His arm drew her closer. Simone, her eyes still closed, drew a deep breath.

"Yes," she murmured, "yes. When your arms are round me I feel safe. I forget my life—the terrible life—of a medium. You know much, Raoul, but even you do not know all it means."

He felt her body grow rigid in his embrace. Her eyes opened again, staring in front of her.

"One sits in the cabinet in the darkness, waiting, and the darkness is terrible, Raoul, for it is the darkness of emptiness, of nothingness. Deliberately one gives oneself up to be lost in it. After that one knows nothing, one feels nothing, but at last there comes the slow, painful return, the awakening out of sleep, but so tired—so terribly tired.''

"I know," murmured Raoul, "I know."

"So tired," murmured Simone again. Her whole body seemed to droop as she repeated the words.

"But you are wonderful, Simone."

He took her hands in his, trying to rouse her to share his enthusiasm.

"You are unique—the greatest medium the world has ever known."

She shook her head, smiling a little at that.

"Yes, yes," Raoul insisted.

He drew two letters from his pocket.

"See here, from Professor Roche of the Salpetriere, and this one from Dr. Genir at Nancy, both imploring that you will continue to sit for them occasionally."

"Ah, no!"

Simone sprang suddenly to her feet.

"I will not, I will not. It is to be all finished—all done with. You promised me, Raoul."

Raoul stared at her in astonishment as she stood wavering, facing him almost like a creature at bay. He got up and took her hand.

"Yes, yes," he said. "Certainly it is finished, that is understood. But I am so proud of you, Simone, that is why I mentioned those letters."

She threw him a swift sideways glance of suspicion.

"It is not that you will ever want me to sit again?"

"No, no," said Raoul, "unless perhaps you yourself would care to, just occasionally for these old friends . . ."

But she interrupted him, speaking excitedly. "No, no, never again. There is danger. I tell you I can feel it, great danger."

She clasped her hands on her forehead a minute, then walked across to the window.

"Promise me never again," she said in a quieter voice over her shoulder.

Raoul followed her and put his arms round her shoulders.

"My dear one," he said tenderly, "I promise you after today you shall never sit again."

He felt the sudden start she gave.

"Today," she murmured. "Ah, yes—I had forgotten Madame Exe."

Raoul looked at his watch. "She is due any minute now; but perhaps, Simone, if you do not feel well . . ."

Simone hardly seemed to be listening to him; she was following out her own train of thought.

"She is—a strange woman, Raoul, a very strange woman. Do you know—I have almost a horror of her."

"Simone!"

There was reproach in his voice, and she was quick to feel it.

"Yes, yes, I know, you are like all Frenchmen, Raoul. To you a mother is sacred and it is unkind of me to feel like that about her when she grieves so for her lost child. But—I cannot explain it, she is so big and black, and her hands—have you ever noticed her hands, Raoul? Great big strong hands, as strong as a man's. Ah!"

She gave a little shiver and closed her eyes. Raoul

withdrew his arm and spoke almost coldly.

"I really cannot understand you, Simone. Surely you, a woman, should have nothing but sympathy for another woman, a mother bereft of her only child."

Simone made a gesture of impatience. "Ah, it is you who do not understand, my friend! One cannot help these things. The first moment I saw her I felt . . ."

She flung her hand out. "Fear! You remember, it was a long time before I would consent to sit for her? I felt sure in some way she would bring me misfortune."

Raoul shrugged his shoulders. "Whereas, in actual fact, she brought you the exact opposite," he said dryly. "All the sittings have been attended with marked success. The spirit of the little Amelie was able to control you at once, and the materializations have really been striking. Professor Roche ought really to have been present at the last one."

"Materializations," said Simone in a low voice. "Tell me, Raoul (you know that I know nothing of what takes place while I am in the trance), are the materializations really so wonderful?"

He nodded enthusiastically. "At the first few sittings the figure of the child was visible in a kind of nebulous haze," he explained, "but at the last séance . . ."

"Yes?"

He spoke very softly. "Simone, the child that stood there was an actual living child of flesh and blood. I even touched her—but seeing that the touch was acutely painful to you, I would not permit

Madame Exe to do the same. I was afraid that her self-control might break down, and that some harm to you might result."

Simone turned away again towards the window.

"I was terribly exhausted when I woke," she murmured. "Raoul, are you sure—are you really sure that all this is right? You know what dear old Elise thinks, that I am trafficking with the devil?" She laughed rather uncertainly.

"You know what I believe," said Raoul gravely. "In the handling of the unknown there must always be danger, but the cause is a noble one, for it is the cause of Science. All over the world there have been martyrs to Science, pioneers who have paid the price so that others may follow safely in their footsteps. For ten years now you have worked for Science at the cost of a terrific nervous strain. Now your part is done, from today onward you are free to be happy."

She smiled at him affectionately, her calm restored. Then she glanced quickly up at the clock.

"Madame Exe is late," she murmured. "She may not come."

"I think she will," said Raoul. "Your clock is a little fast, Simone."

Simone moved about the room, rearranging an ornament here and there.

"I wonder who she is, this Madame Exe?" she observed. "Where she comes from, who her people are? It is strange that we know nothing about her."

Raoul shrugged his shoulders. "Most people remain incognito if possible when they come to a medium," he observed. "It is an elementary precaution."

"I suppose so," agreed Simone listlessly.

A little china vase she was holding slipped from her fingers and broke to pieces on the tiles of the fireplace. She turned sharply on Raoul.

"You see," she murmured, "I am not myself. Raoul, would you think me very—very cowardly if I told Madame Exe I could not sit today?"

His look of pained astonishment made her redden.

"You promised, Simone . . ." he began gently.

She backed against the wall. "I won't do it, Raoul. I won't do it."

And again that glance of his, tenderly reproachful, made her wince.

"It is not of the money I am thinking, Simone, though you must realize that the money this woman has offered you for a last sitting is enormous—simply enormous."

She interrupted him defiantly. "There are things that matter more than money."

"Certainly there are," he agreed warmly. "That is just what I am saying. Consider—this woman is a mother, a mother who has lost her only child. If you are not really ill, if it is only a whim on your part —you can deny a rich woman a caprice, but can you deny a mother one last sight of her child?"

The medium flung her hands out despairingly in front of her.

"Oh, you torture me," she murmured. "All the same you are right. I will do as you wish, but I know now what I am afraid of—it is the word 'mother.' "

"Simone!"

"There are certain primitive elementary forces, Raoul. Most of them have been destroyed by civilization, but motherhood stands where it stood at the beginning. Animals—human beings, they are all the same. A mother's love for her child is like nothing else in the world. It knows no law, no pity, it dares all things and crushes down remorselessly all that stands in its path.''

She stopped, panting a little, then turned to him with a quick, disarming smile.

''I am foolish today, Raoul. I know it.''

He took her hand in his. ''Lie down for a minute or two,'' he urged. ''Rest till she comes.''

''Very well.'' She smiled at him and left the room. Raoul remained for a minute or two lost in thought, then he strode to the door, opened it, and crossed the little hall. He went into a room the other side of it, a sitting-room very much like the one he had left, but at one end was an alcove with a big armchair set in it. Heavy black velvet curtains were arranged so as to pull across the alcove. Elise was busy arranging the room. Close to the alcove she had set two chairs and a small round table. On the table was a tambourine, a horn, and some paper and pencils.

''The last time,'' murmured Elise with grim satisfaction. ''Ah, monsieur, I wish it were over and done with.''

The sharp ting of an electric bell sounded.

''There she is, that great *gendarme* of a woman,'' continued the old servant. ''Why can't she go and pray decently for her little one's soul in a church, and burn a candle to Our Blessed Lady? Does not the good God know what is best for us?''

''Answer the bell, Elise,'' said Raoul peremptorily. She threw him a look, but obeyed. In a minute or two she returned ushering in the visitor.

"I will tell my mistress you are here, madame."

Raoul came forward to shake hands with Madame Exe. Simone's words floated back to his memory.

"So big and so black."

She was a big woman, and the heavy black of French mourning seemed almost exaggerated in her case. Her voice when she spoke was very deep.

"I fear I am a little late, monsieur."

"A few minutes only," said Raoul, smiling. "Madame Simone is lying down. I am sorry to say she is far from well, very nervous and overwrought."

Her hand, which she was just withdrawing, closed on his suddenly like a vise.

"But she will sit?" she demanded sharply.

"Oh, yes, madame."

Madame Exe gave a sigh of relief, and sank into a chair, loosening one of the heavy black veils that floated round her.

"Ah, monsieur!" she murmured, "you cannot imagine, you cannot conceive the wonder and the joy of these séances to me! My little one! My Amelie! To see her, to hear her, even—perhaps—yes, perhaps to be even able to—stretch out my hand and touch her."

Raoul spoke quickly and peremptorily. "Madame Exe—how can I explain?—on no account must you do anything except under my express directions, otherwise there is the gravest danger."

"Danger to me?"

"No, madame," said Raoul, "to the medium. You must understand that the phenomena that occur are explained by Science in a certain way. I will put the matter very simply, using no technical terms. A spirit, to manifest itself, has to use the actual physical substance of the medium. You have seen the vapor of fluid issuing from the lips of the medium. This finally condenses and is built up into the physical semblance of the spirit's dead body. But this ectoplasm we believe to be the actual substance of the medium. We hope to prove this some day by careful weighing and testing—but the great difficulty is the danger and pain which attends the medium on any handling of the phenomena. Were anyone to seize hold of the materialization roughly, the death of the medium might result."

Madame Exe had listened to him with close attention.

"That is very interesting, monsieur. Tell me, shall not a time come when the materialization shall advance so far that it shall be capable of detachment from its parent, the medium?"

"That is a fantastic speculation, madame."

She persisted. "But, on the facts, not impossible?"

"Quite impossible today."

"But perhaps in the future?"

He was saved from answering, for at that moment Simone entered. She looked languid and pale, but had evidently regained entire control of herself. She came forward and shook hands with Madame Exe, though Raoul noticed the faint shiver that passed through her as she did so.

"I regret, madame, to hear that you are indisposed," said Madame Exe.

"It is nothing," said Simone rather brusquely. "Shall we begin?"

She went to the alcove and sat down in the armchair. Suddenly Raoul in his turn felt a wave of fear pass over him.

"You are not strong enough," he exclaimed. "We had better cancel the séance. Madame Exe will understand."

"Monsieur!"

Madame Exe rose indignantly.

"Yes, yes, it is better not, I am sure of it."

"Madame Simone promised me one last sitting."

"That is so," agreed Simone quietly, "and I am prepared to carry out my promise."

"I hold you to it, madame," said the other woman.

"I do not break my word," said Simone coldly. "Do not fear, Raoul," she added gently, "after all, it is for the last time—the last time, thank God."

At a sign from her Raoul drew the heavy black curtains across the alcove. He also pulled the curtains of the window so that the room was in semi-obscurity. He indicated one of the chairs to Madame Exe and prepared himself to take the other. Madame Exe, however, hesitated.

"You will pardon me, monsieur, but—you understand I believe absolutely in your integrity and in that of Madame Simone. All the same, so that my testimony may be the more valuable, I took the liberty of bringing this with me."

From her handbag she drew a length of fine cord.

"Madame!" cried Raoul. "This is an insult!"

"A precaution."

"I repeat it is an insult."

"I don't understand your objection, monsieur," said Madame Exe coldly. "If there is no trickery you have nothing to fear."

Raoul laughed scornfully. "I can assure you that I have nothing to fear, madame. Bind me hand and foot if you will."

His speech did not produce the effect he hoped, for Madame Exe merely murmured unemotionally:

"Thank you, monsieur," and advanced upon him with her roll of cord.

Suddenly Simone from behind the curtain gave a cry.

"No, no, Raoul, don't let her do it."

Madame Exe laughed derisively. "Madame is afraid," she observed sarcastically.

"Yes, I am afraid."

"Remember what you are saying, Simone," cried Raoul. "Madame Exe is apparently under the impression that we are charlatans."

"I must make sure," said Madame Exe grimly.

She went methodically about her task, binding Raoul securely to his chair.

"I must congratulate you on your knots, madame," he observed ironically when she had finished. "Are you satisfied now?"

Madame Exe did not reply. She walked round the room examining the panelling of the walls closely. Then she locked the door leading into the hall, and, removing the key, returned to her chair.

"Now," she said in an indescribable voice. "I am ready."

The minutes passed. From behind the curtain the sound of Simone's breathing became heavier and more stertorous. Then it died away altogether, to be succeeded by a series of moans. Then again there was silence for a little while, broken by the sudden clattering of the tambourine. The horn was caught up from the table and dashed to the ground. Ironic laughter was heard. The curtains of the alcove seemed to have been pulled back a little, the medium's figure was just visible through the opening, her head fallen forward on her breast. Suddenly Madame Exe drew in her breath sharply. A ribbon-like stream of mist was issuing from the medium's mouth. It condensed and began gradually to assume a shape, the shape of a little child.

"Amelie! My little Amelie!"

The hoarse whisper came from Madame Exe. The hazy figure condensed still further. Raoul stared almost incredulously. Never had there been a more successful materialization. Now, surely it was a real child, a real flesh and blood child standing there.

"Maman!" The soft childish voice spoke.

"My child!" cried Madame Exe. "My child!" She half-rose from her seat.

"Be careful, madame," cried Raoul warningly.

The materialization came hesitatingly through the curtains. It was a child. She stood there, her arms held out.

"Maman!"

"Ah!" cried Madame Exe. Again she half-rose from her seat.

"Madame," cried Raoul, alarmed, "the medium . . ."

"I must touch her," cried Madame Exe hoarsely.

She moved a step forward.

"For God's sake, madame, control yourself," cried Raoul.

He was really alarmed now.

"Sit down at once."

"My little one, I must touch her."

"Madame, I command you, sit down!"

He was writhing desperately with his bonds, but Madame Exe had done her work well; he was helpless. A terrible sense of impending disaster swept over him.

"In the name of God, madame, sit down!" he shouted. "Remember the medium."

Madame Exe paid no attention to him. She was like a woman transformed. Ecstasy and delight showed plainly in her face. Her outstretched hand touched the little figure that stood in the opening of the curtains. A terrible moan came from the medium.

"My God!" cried Raoul. "My God! This is terrible. The medium . . ."

Madame Exe turned on him with a harsh laugh.

"What do I care for your medium?" she cried. "I want my child."

"You are mad!"

"My child, I tell you. Mine! My own flesh and blood! My little one come back to me from the dead, alive and breathing."

Raoul opened his lips, but no words would come. She was terrible, this woman! Remorseless, savage, absorbed by her own passion. The baby lips parted, and for the third time the same word echoed:

"Maman!"

"Come then, my little one," cried Madame Exe.

With a sharp gesture she caught up the child in her arms. From behind the curtains came a long-drawn scream of utter anguish.

"Simone!" cried Raoul. "Simone!"

He was aware vaguely of Madame Exe rushing past him, of the unlocking of the door, of retreating footsteps down the stairs.

From behind the curtain there still sounded the terrible, high, long-drawn scream, such a scream, as Raoul had never heard. It died away in a horrible kind of gurgle. Then there came the thud of a body falling. . . .

Raoul was working like a maniac to free himself from his bonds. In his frenzy he accomplished the impossible, snapping the rope by sheer strength. As he struggled to his feet, Elise rushed in, crying, "Madame!"

"Simone!" cried Raoul.

Together they rushed forward and pulled the curtain. Raoul staggered back.

"My God!" he murmured. "Red—all red. . . ."

Elise's voice came beside him harsh and shaking.

"So Madame is dead. It is ended. But tell me, monsieur, what has happened. Why is Madame all shrunken away—why is she half her usual size? What has been happening here?"

"I do not know," said Raoul.

His voice rose to a scream.

"I do not know. I do not know. But I think—I am going mad. . . . Simone! Simone!"

Sanctuary

The Vicar's wife came round the corner of the Vicarage with her arms full of chrysanthemums. A good deal of rich garden soil was attached to her strong brogue shoes and a few fragments of earth were adhering to her nose, but of that fact she was perfectly unconscious.

She had a slight struggle in opening the Vicarage gate which hung, rustily, half off its hinges. A puff of wind caught at her battered felt hat, causing it to sit even more rakishly than it had done before. "Bother!" said Bunch.

Christened by her optimistic parents Diana, Mrs. Harmon had become Bunch at an early age for somewhat obvious reasons and the name had stuck to her ever since. Clutching the chrysanthemums, she made her way through the gate to the churchyard, and so to the church door.

The November air was mild and damp. Clouds

185

scudded across the sky with patches of blue here and there. Inside, the church was dark and cold; it was unheated except at service times.

"Brrrrrh!" said Bunch expressively. "I'd better get on with this quickly. I don't want to die of cold."

With the quickness born of practice she collected the necessary paraphernalia: vases, water, flower-holders. "I wish we had lilies," thought Bunch to herself. "I get so tired of these scraggy chrysanthemums." Her nimble fingers arranged the blooms in their holders.

There was nothing particularly original or artistic about the decorations, for Bunch Harmon herself was neither original nor artistic, but it was a homely and pleasant arrangement. Carrying the vases carefully, Bunch stepped up the aisle and made her way toward the altar. As she did so the sun came out.

It shone through the East window of somewhat crude colored glass, mostly blue and red—the gift of a wealthy Victorian churchgoer. The effect was almost startling in its sudden opulence. "Like jewels," thought Bunch. Suddenly she stopped, staring ahead of her. On the chancel steps was a huddled dark form.

Putting down the flowers carefully, Bunch went up to it and bent over it. It was a man lying there, huddled over on himself. Bunch knelt down by him and slowly, carefully, she turned him over. Her fingers went to his pulse—a pulse so feeble and fluttering that it told its own story, as did the almost greenish pallor of his face. There was no doubt, Bunch thought, that the man was dying.

He was a man of about forty-five, dressed in a

dark, shabby suit. She laid down the limp hand she had picked up and looked at his other hand. This seemed clenched like a fist on his breast. Looking more closely she saw that the fingers were closed over what seemed to be a large wad or handkerchief which he was holding tightly to his chest. All round the clenched hand there were splashes of a dry brown fluid which, Bunch guessed, was dry blood. Bunch sat back on her heels, frowning.

Up till now the man's eyes had been closed but at this point they suddenly opened and fixed themselves on Bunch's face. They were neither dazed nor wandering. They seemed fully alive and intelligent. His lips moved, and Bunch bent forward to catch the words, or rather the word. It was only one word that he said:

"Sanctuary."

There was, she thought, just a very faint smile as he breathed out this word. There was no mistaking it, for after a moment, he said it again, "Sanctuary . . ."

Then, with a faint, long-drawn-out sigh, his eyes closed again. Once more Bunch's fingers went to his pulse. It was still there, but fainter now and more intermittent. She got up with decision.

"Don't move," she said, "or try to move. I'm going for help."

The man's eyes opened again but he seemed now to be fixing his attention on the colored light that came through the East window. He murmured something that Bunch could not quite catch. She thought, startled, that it might have been her husband's name.

"Julian?" she said. "Did you come here to find Julian?" But there was no answer. The man lay with eyes closed, his breathing coming in slow, shallow fashion.

Bunch turned and left the church rapidly. She glanced at her watch and nodded with some satisfaction. Dr. Griffiths would still be in his surgery. It was only a couple of minutes' walk from the church. She went in, without waiting to knock or ring, passing through the waiting room and into the doctor's surgery.

"You must come at once," said Bunch. "There's a man dying in the church."

Some minutes later Dr. Griffiths rose from his knees after a brief examination.

"Can we move him from here into the Vicarage? I can attend to him better there—not that it's any use."

"Of course," said Bunch. "I'll go along and get things ready. I'll get Harper and Jones, shall I? To help you carry him."

"Thanks. I can telephone from the Vicarage for an ambulance, but I'm afraid—by the time it comes . . ." He left the remark unfinished.

Bunch said, "Internal bleeding?"

Dr. Griffiths nodded. He said, "How on earth did he come here?"

"I think he must have been here all night," said Bunch, considering. "Harper unlocks the church in the morning as he goes to work, but he doesn't usually come in."

It was about five minutes later when Dr. Griffiths put down the telephone receiver and came back into the morning room where the injured man was lying on quickly arranged blankets on the sofa. Bunch was moving a basin of water and clearing up after the doctor's examination.

"Well, that's that," said Griffiths. "I've sent for an ambulance and I've notified the police." He stood, frowning, looking down on the patient who lay with closed eyes. His left hand was plucking in a nervous, spasmodic way at his side.

"He was shot," said Griffiths. "Shot at fairly close quarters. He rolled his handkerchief up into a ball and plugged the wound with it so as to stop the bleeding."

"Could he have gone far after that happened?" Bunch asked.

"Oh, yes, it's quite possible. A mortally wounded man has been known to pick himself up and walk along a street as though nothing had happened, and then suddenly collapse five or ten minutes later. So he needn't have been shot in the church. Oh, no. He may have been shot some distance away. Of course, he may have shot himself and then dropped the revolver and staggered blindly toward the church. I don't quite know why he made for the church and not for the Vicarage."

"Oh, I know *that*," said Bunch. "He said it: 'Sanctuary.' "

The doctor stared at her. "Sanctuary?"

"Here's Julian," said Bunch, turning her head as she heard her husband's steps in the hall. "Julian! Come here."

The Reverend Julian Harmon entered the room. His vague, scholarly manner always made him appear much older than he really was. "Dear me!" said Julian Harmon, staring in a mild, puzzled manner at the surgical appliances and the prone figure on the sofa.

Bunch explained with her usual economy of words. "He was in the church, dying. He'd been shot. Do you know him, Julian? I thought he said your name."

The Vicar came up to the sofa and looked down at the dying man. "Poor fellow," he said, and shook his head. "No, I don't know him. I'm almost sure I've never seen him before."

At that moment the dying man's eyes opened once more. They went from the doctor to Julian Harmon and from him to his wife. The eyes stayed there, staring into Bunch's face. Griffiths stepped forward.

"If you could tell us," he said urgently.

But with his eyes fixed on Bunch, the man said in a weak voice, "Please—*please*—" And then, with a slight tremor, he died . . .

Sergeant Hayes licked his pencil and turned the page of his notebook.

"So that's all you can tell me, Mrs. Harmon?"

"That's all," said Bunch. "These are the things out of his coat pockets."

On a table at Sergeant Hayes' elbow was a wallet, a rather battered old watch with the initials W.S. and the return half of a ticket to London. Nothing more.

"You've found out who he is?" asked Bunch.

"A Mr. and Mrs. Eccles phoned up the station. He's her brother, it seems. Name of Sandbourne. Been in a low state of health and nerves for some time. He's been getting worse lately. The day before yesterday he walked out and didn't come back. He took a revolver with him."

"And he came out here and shot himself with it?" said Bunch. "Why?"

"Well, you see, he'd been depressed . . ."

Bunch interrupted him. "I don't mean *that*. I mean, why here?"

Since Sergeant Hayes obviously did not know the answer to that one he replied in an oblique fashion, "Come out here, he did, on the 5:10 bus."

"Yes," said Bunch again. "But *why*?"

"I don't know, Mrs. Harmon," said Sergeant Hayes. "There's no accounting. If the balance of the mind is disturbed—"

Bunch finished for him. "They may do it anywhere. But it still seems to me unnecessary to take a bus out to a small country place like this. He didn't know anyone here, did he?"

"Not so far as can be ascertained," said Sergeant Hayes. He coughed in an apologetic manner and said, as he rose to his feet, "It may be as Mr. and Mrs. Eccles will come out and see you, Ma'am—if you don't mind, that is."

"Of course I don't mind," said Bunch. "It's very natural. I only wish I had something to tell them."

"I'll be getting along," said Sergeant Hayes.

"I'm only so thankful," said Bunch, going with him to the front door, "that it wasn't murder."

A car had drawn up at the Vicarage gate. Sergeant Hayes, glancing at it, remarked: "Looks as though that's Mr. and Mrs. Eccles come here now, Ma'am, to talk with you."

Bunch braced herself to endure what, she felt, might be rather a difficult ordeal. "However," she thought, "I can always call Julian in to help me. A clergyman's a great help when people are bereaved."

Exactly what she had expected Mr. and Mrs. Eccles to be like, Bunch could not have said, but she was conscious, as she greeted them, of a feeling of surprise. Mr. Eccles was a stout and florid man whose natural manner would have been cheerful and facetious. Mrs. Eccles had a vaguely flashy look about her. She had a small, mean, pursed-up mouth. Her voice was thin and reedy.

"It's been a terrible shock, Mrs. Harmon, as you can imagine," she said.

"Oh, I know," said Bunch. "It must have been. Do sit down. Can I offer you—well, perhaps it's a little early for tea—"

Mr. Eccles waved a pudgy hand. "No, no, nothing for us," he said. "It's very kind of you, I'm sure. Just wanted to . . . well . . . what poor William said and all that, you know?"

"He's been abroad a long time," said Mrs. Eccles, "and I think he must have had some very nasty experiences. Very quiet and depressed he's been, ever since he came home. Said the world wasn't fit to live in and there was nothing to look forward to. Poor Bill, he was always moody."

Bunch stared at them both for a moment or two without speaking.

"Pinched my husband's revolver, he did," went on Mrs. Eccles. "Without our knowing. Then it seems he come out here by bus. I suppose that was nice feeling on his part. He wouldn't have liked to do it in our house."

"Poor fellow, poor fellow," said Mr. Eccles, with a sigh. "It doesn't do to judge."

There was another short pause, and Mr. Eccles

said, "Did he leave a message? Any last words, nothing like that?"

His bright, rather piglike eyes watched Bunch closely. Mrs. Eccles, too, leaned forward as though anxious for the reply.

"No," said Bunch quietly. "He came into the church when he was dying, for sanctuary."

Mrs. Eccles said in a puzzled voice, "Sanctuary? I don't think I quite . . ."

Mr. Eccles interrupted. "Holy place, my dear," he said impatiently. "That's what the Vicar's wife means. It's a sin—suicide, you know. I expect he wanted to make amends."

"He tried to say something just before he died," said Bunch. "He began, 'Please,' but that's as far as he got." Mrs. Eccles put her handkerchief to her eyes and sniffed.

"Oh, dear," she said. "It's terribly upsetting, isn't it?"

"There, there, Pam," said her husband. "Don't take on. These things can't be helped. Poor Willie. Still, he's at peace now. Well, thank you very much, Mrs. Harmon. I hope we haven't interrupted you. A vicar's wife is a busy lady, we know that."

They shook hands with her. Then Eccles turned back suddenly to say, "Oh, yes, there's just one thing. I think you've got his coat here, haven't you?"

"His coat?" Bunch frowned.

Mrs. Eccles said, "We'd like all his things, you know. Sentimental-like."

"He had a watch and a wallet and a railway ticket in the pockets," said Bunch. "I gave them to Sergeant Hayes."

"That's all right, then," said Mr. Eccles. "He'll

hand them over to us, I expect. His private papers would be in the wallet."

"There was a pound note in the wallet," said Bunch. "Nothing else."

"No letters? Nothing like that?"

Bunch shook her head.

"Well, thank you again, Mrs. Harmon. The coat he was wearing—perhaps the Sergeant's got that too, has he?"

Bunch frowned in an effort of remembrance.

"No," she said. "I don't think . . . let me see. The doctor and I took his coat off to examine his wound." She looked round the room, vaguely. "I must have taken it upstairs with the towels and basin."

"I wonder now, Mrs. Harmon, if you don't mind . . . We'd like his coat, you know, the last thing he wore. Well, the wife feels rather sentimental about it."

"Of course," said Bunch. "Would you like me to have it cleaned first? I'm afraid it's rather—well—stained."

"Oh, no, no, no, that doesn't matter."

Bunch frowned. "Now I wonder where . . . excuse me a moment." She went upstairs and it was some few minutes before she returned.

"I'm so sorry," she said breathlessly, "my daily woman must have put it aside with other clothes that were going to the cleaners. It's taken me quite a long time to find it. Here it is. I'll do it up for you in brown paper."

Disclaiming their protests she did so; then once more effusively bidding her farewell the Eccles departed.

Bunch went slowly back across the hall and entered the study. The Reverend Julian Harmon looked up and his brow cleared. He was composing a sermon and was fearing that he'd been led astray by the interest of the political relations between Judaea and Persia, in the reign of Cyrus.

"Yes, dear?" he said, hopefully.

"Julian," said Bunch. "What's *Sanctuary* exactly?"

Julian Harmon gratefully put aside his sermon paper.

"Well," he said. "Sanctuary in Roman and Greek temples applied to the *cella* in which stood the statue of a god. The Latin word for altar '*ara*' also means protection." He continued learnedly: "In 399 A.D. the right of sanctuary in Christian churches was finally and definitely recognized. The earliest mention of the right of sanctuary in England is in the Code of Laws issued by Ethelbert in A.D. 600 . . ."

He continued for some time with his exposition but was, as often, disconcerted by his wife's reception of his erudite pronouncement.

"Darling," she said. "You *are* sweet."

Bending over, she kissed him on the tip of his nose. Julian felt rather like a dog who has been congratulated on performing a clever trick.

"The Eccles have been here," said Bunch.

The Vicar frowned. "The Eccles? I don't seem to remember . . ."

"You don't know them. They're the sister and her husband of the man in the church."

"My dear, you ought to have called me."

"There wasn't any need," said Bunch. "They were not in need of consolation. I wonder now." She frowned. "If I put a casserole in the oven tomorrow, can you manage, Julian? I think I shall have to go up to London for the sales."

"The sails?" Her husband looked at her blankly. "Do you mean a yacht or a boat or something?"

Bunch laughed.

"No, darling. There's a special white sale at Burrows and Portman's. You know, sheets, table-cloths and towels and glass-cloths. I don't know what we do with our glass-cloths, the way they wear through. Besides," she added thoughtfully, "I think I ought to go and see Aunt Jane."

That sweet old lady, Miss Jane Marple, was enjoying the delights of the metropolis for a fortnight, comfortably installed in her nephew's studio flat.

"So kind of dear Raymond," she murmured. "He and Joan have gone to America for a fortnight and they insisted I should come up here and enjoy myself. And now, dear Bunch, do tell me what it is that's worrying you."

Bunch was Miss Marple's favorite godchild, and the old lady looked at her with great affection as Bunch, thrusting her best felt hat further on the back of her head, started on her story.

Bunch's recital was concise and clear. Miss Marple nodded her head as Bunch finished. "I see," she said. "Yes, I see."

"That's why I felt I had to see you," said Bunch. "You see, not being clever—"

"But you *are* clever, my dear."

"No, I'm not. Not clever like Julian."

"Julian, of course, has a very solid intellect," said Miss Marple.

"That's it," said Bunch. "Julian's got the intellect, but on the other hand, I've got the *sense*."

"You have a lot of common sense, Bunch, and you're very intelligent."

"You see, I don't really know what I ought to do. I can't ask Julian because—well, I mean, Julian's so full of rectitude . . ."

This statement appeared to be perfectly understood by Miss Marple, who said, "I know what you mean, dear. We women—well, it's different." She went on, "You told me what happened, Bunch, but I'd like to know first exactly what you think."

"It's all wrong," said Bunch. "The man who was there in the church, dying, knew all about Sanctuary. He said it just the way Julian would have said it. I mean he was a well-read, educated man. And if he'd shot himself, he wouldn't drag himself into a church afterward and say 'sanctuary.' Sanctuary means that you're pursued, and when you get into a church you're safe. Your pursuers can't touch you. At one time even the law couldn't get at you."

She looked questioningly at Miss Marple. The latter nodded. Bunch went on, "Those people, the Eccles, were quite different. Ignorant and coarse. And there's another thing. That watch—the dead man's watch. It had the initials W.S. on the back of it. But inside—I opened it—in very small lettering there was "To Walter from his father" and a date. *Walter*. But the Eccles kept talking of him as William or Bill."

Miss Marple seemed about to speak but Bunch rushed on, "Oh, I know you're not always called the name you're baptized by. I mean, I can understand that you might be christened William and called 'Porky' or 'Carrots' or something. But your sister wouldn't call you William or Bill if your name was Walter.''

"You mean that she wasn't his sister?''

"I'm quite sure she wasn't his sister. They were horrid—both of them. They came to the Vicarage to get his things and to find out if he'd said anything before he died. When I said he hadn't I saw it in their faces—relief. I think, myself,'' finished Bunch, "it was Eccles who shot him.''

"Murder?'' said Miss Marple.

"Yes,'' said Bunch. "Murder. That's why I came to you, darling.''

Bunch's remark might have seemed incongruous to an ignorant listener, but in certain spheres Miss Marple had a reputation for dealing with murder.

"He said 'please' to me before he died,'' said Bunch. "He wanted me to do something for him. The awful thing is I've no idea what.''

Miss Marple considered for a moment or two, and then pounced on the point that had already occurred to Bunch. "But why was he there at all?'' she asked.

"You mean,'' said Bunch, "if you wanted sanctuary you might pop into a church anywhere. There's no need to take a bus that only goes four times a day and come out to a lonely spot like ours for it.''

"He must have come there for a purpose,'' Miss Marple thought. "He must have come to see someone. Chipping Cleghorn's not a big place, Bunch. Surely you must have some idea of who it was he came to see?''

Bunch reviewed the inhabitants of her village in her mind before rather doubtfully shaking her head.

"In a way," she said, "it could be anybody."

"He never mentioned a name?"

"He said Julian, or I thought he said Julian. It might have been Julia, I suppose. As far as I know, there isn't any Julia living in Chipping Cleghorn."

She screwed up her eyes as she thought back to the scene. The man lying there on the chancel steps, the light coming through the window with its jewels of red and blue light.

"Jewels," said Bunch suddenly. "Perhaps that's what he said. The light coming through the East window looked like jewels."

"Jewels," said Miss Marple, thoughtfully.

"I'm coming now," said Bunch, "to the most important thing of all. The reason why I've really come here today. You see, the Eccles made a great fuss about having his coat. We took it off when the doctor was seeing to him. It was an old, shabby sort of coat—there was no reason they should have wanted it. They pretended it was sentimental, but that was nonsense.

"Anyway, I went up to find it, and as I was going up the stairs I remembered how he'd made a kind of picking gesture with his hand, as though he was fumbling with the coat. So when I got hold of the coat I looked at it very carefully and I saw that in one place the lining had been sewn up again with a different thread. So I unpicked it and I found a little piece of paper inside. I took it out and I sewed it up again properly with thread that matched. I was careful and I don't really think that the Eccles would know I've done it. I don't *think* so, but I can't be sure. And I took the coat down to them and made some excuse for the delay."

"The piece of paper?" asked Miss Marple.

Bunch opened her handbag. "I didn't show it to Julian," she said, "because he would have said that I ought to have given it to the Eccles. But I thought I'd rather bring it to you instead."

"A cloakroom ticket," said Miss Marple, looking at it. "Paddington Station."

"He had a return ticket to Paddington in his pocket," said Bunch.

The eyes of the two women met.

"This calls for action," said Miss Marple briskly. "But it would be advisable, I think, to be careful. Would you have noticed at all, Bunch dear, whether you were followed when you came to London to-day?"

"Followed!" exclaimed Bunch. "You don't think—"

"Well, I think it's *possible*," said Miss Marple. "When anything is possible, I think we ought to take precautions." She rose with a brisk movement. "You came up here ostensibly, my dear, to go to the sales. I think the right thing to do, therefore, would be for us to *go* to the sales. But before we set out, we might put one or two little arrangements in hand. I don't suppose," Miss Marple added obscurely, "that I shall need the old speckled tweed with the beaver collar just at present. . . ."

It was about an hour and a half later that the two ladies, rather the worse for wear and battered in appearance, and both clasping parcels of hardly-won household linen, sat down at a small and sequestered hostelry called the Apple Bough to restore their forces with steak and kidney pudding followed by apple tart and custard.

"Really a prewar quality face towel," gasped Miss Marple, slightly out of breath. "With a J on it, too. So fortunate that Raymond's wife's name is Joan. I shall put them aside until I really need them and then they will do for her if I pass on sooner than I expect."

"I really did need the glass-cloths," said Bunch. "And they were very cheap, though not as cheap as the ones that woman with the ginger hair managed to snatch from me."

A smart young woman with a lavish application of rouge and lipstick entered the Apple Bough at that moment. After looking round vaguely for a moment or two, she hurried to their table. She laid down an envelope by Miss Marple's elbow.

"There you are, Miss," she said briskly.

"Oh, thank you, Gladys," said Miss Marple. "Thank you very much. So kind of you."

"Always pleased to oblige, I'm sure," said Gladys. "Ernie always says to me 'Everything what's good you learned from that Miss Marple of yours that you were in service with,' and I'm sure I'm always glad to oblige you, Miss."

"Such a dear girl," said Miss Marple as Gladys departed again. "Always so willing and so kind."

She looked inside the envelope and then passed it on to Bunch. "Now be very careful, dear," she said. "By the way, is there still that nice young Inspector at Melchester that I remember?"

"I don't know," said Bunch. "I expect so."

"Well, if not," said Miss Marple, thoughtfully, "I can always ring up the Chief Constable. I *think* he would remember me."

"Of course he'd remember you," said Bunch.

"Everybody would remember *you*. You're quite unique." She rose.

Arrived at Paddington, Bunch went to the Luggage Office and produced the cloakroom ticket. A moment or two later a rather shabby old suitcase was passed across to her, and carrying this she made her way to the platform.

The journey home was uneventful. Bunch rose as the train approached Chipping Cleghorn and picked up the old suitcase. She had just left her carriage when a man, sprinting along the platform, suddenly seized the suitcase from her hand and rushed off with it.

"Stop!" Bunch yelled. "Stop him, stop him. He's taken my suitcase."

The ticket collector who, at this rural station, was a man of somewhat slow processes, had just begun to say, "Now, look here, you can't do that—" when a smart blow in the chest pushed him aside, and the man with the suitcase rushed out from the station. He made his way toward a waiting car. Tossing the suitcase in, he was about to climb after it but before he could move a hand fell on his shoulder, and the voice of Police Constable Abel said, "Now then, what's all this?"

Bunch arrived, panting, from the station. "He snatched my suitcase," she said.

"Nonsense," said the man. "I don't know what this lady means. It's my suitcase. I just got out of the train with it."

"Now, let's get this clear," said Police Constable Abel.

He looked at Bunch with a bovine and impartial

stare. Nobody would have guessed that Police Constable Abel and Mrs. Harmon spent long half hours in Police Constable Abel's off time discussing the respective merits of manure and bone meal for rose bushes.

"You say, Madam, that this is your suitcase?" said Police Constable Abel.

"Yes," said Bunch. "Definitely."

"And you, sir?"

"I say this suitcase is mine."

The man was tall, dark and well dressed, with a drawling voice and a superior manner. A feminine voice from inside the car, said, "Of course it's your suitcase, Edwin. I don't know what this woman means."

"We'll have to get this clear," said Police Constable Abel. "If it's your suitcase, Madam, what do you say is inside it?"

"Clothes," said Bunch. "A long speckled coat with a beaver collar, two wool jumpers and a pair of shoes."

"Well, that's clear enough," said Police Constable Abel. He turned to the other.

"I am a theatrical costumer," said the dark man importantly. "This suitcase contains theatrical properties which I brought down here for an amateur performance."

"Right, sir," said Police Constable Abel. "Well, we'll just look inside, shall we, and see? We can go along to the police station, or if you're in a hurry we'll take the suitcase back to the station and open it there."

"It'll suit me," said the dark man. "My name is

Moss, by the way. Edwin Moss."

The Police Constable, holding the suitcase, went back into the station. "Just taking this into the Parcels Office, George," he said to the ticket collector.

Police Constable Abel laid the suitcase on the counter of the Parcels Office and pushed back the clasp. The case was not locked. Bunch and Mr. Edwin Moss stood on either side of him, their eyes regarding each other vengefully.

"Ah!" said Police Constable Abel, as he pushed up the lid.

Inside, neatly folded, was a long rather shabby tweed coat with a beaver fur collar. There were also two wool jumpers and a pair of country shoes.

"Exactly as you say, Madam," said Police Constable Abel, turning to Bunch.

Nobody could have said that Mr. Edwin Moss underdid things. His dismay and compunction were magnificent.

"I do apologize," he said. "I really *do* apologize. Please believe me, dear lady, when I tell you how very, very sorry I am. Unpardonable—quite unpardonable—my behavior has been." He looked at his watch. "I must rush now. Probably my suitcase has gone on the train." Raising his hat once more, he said meltingly to Bunch, "Do, *do* forgive me," and rushed hurriedly out of the Parcels Office.

"Are you going to let him get away?" asked Bunch in a conspiratorial whisper of Police Constable Abel.

The latter slowly closed a bovine eye in a wink.

"He won't get too far, Ma'am," he said. "That's to say, he won't get far unobserved, if you take my meaning."

"Oh," said Bunch, relieved.

"That old lady's been on the phone," said Police Constable Abel, "the one as was down here a few years ago. Bright she is, isn't she? But there's been a lot cooking up all today. Shouldn't wonder if the Inspector or Sergeant was out to see you about it tomorrow morning."

It was the Inspector who came, the Inspector Craddock whom Miss Marple remembered. He greeted Bunch with a smile as an old friend.

"Crime in Chipping Cleghorn again," he said cheerfully. "You don't lack for sensation here, do you, Mrs. Harmon?"

"I could do with rather less," said Bunch. "Have you come to ask me questions or are you going to tell me things for a change?"

"I'll tell you some things first," said the Inspector. "To begin with, Mr. and Mrs. Eccles have been having an eye kept on them for some time. There's reason to believe they've been connected with several robberies in this part of the world. For another thing, although Mrs. Eccles *has* a brother called Sandbourne who has recently come back from abroad, the man you found dying in the church yesterday was definitely not Sandbourne."

"I knew that he wasn't," said Bunch. "His name was Walter, to begin with, not William."

The Inspector nodded. "His name was Walter St. John, and he escaped forty-eight hours ago from Charrington Prison."

"Of course," said Bunch softly to herself, "he was being hunted down by the law, and he took sanctuary." Then she asked, "What had he done?"

"I'll have to go back rather a long way. It's a complicated story. Several years ago there was a certain dancer doing turns at the music halls. I don't expect you'll have ever heard of her, but she specialized in an Arabian Night turn, 'Aladdin in the Cave of Jewels' it was called. She wore bits of rhinestone and not much else.

"She wasn't much of a dancer, I believe, but she was—well—attractive. Anyway, a certain Asiatic royalty fell for her in a big way. Amongst other things he gave her a very magnificent emerald necklace."

"The historic jewels of a Rajah?" murmured Bunch ecstatically.

Inspector Craddock coughed. "Well, a rather more modern version, Mrs. Harmon. The affair didn't last very long, broke up when our potentate's attention was captured by a certain film star whose demands were not quite so modest.

"Zobeida, to give the dancer her stage name, hung on to the necklace, and in due course it was stolen. It disappeared from her dressing room at the theater, and there was a lingering suspicion in the minds of the authorities that she herself might have engineered its disappearance. Such things have been known as a publicity stunt, or indeed from more dishonest motives.

"The necklace was never recovered, but during the course of the investigation the attention of the police was drawn to this man, Walter St. John. He was a man of education and breeding who had come down in the world, and who was employed as a working

jeweler with a rather obscure firm which was suspected as acting as a fence for jewel robberies.

"There was evidence that this necklace had passed
through his hands. It was, however, in connection
with the theft of some other jewelry that he was finally brought to trial and convicted and sent to
prison. He had not very much longer to serve, so his
escape was rather a surprise."

"But why did he come here?" asked Bunch.

"We'd like to know that very much, Mrs. Harmon. Following up his trail, it seems that he went
first to London. He didn't visit any of his old
associates but he visited an elderly woman, a Mrs.
Jacobs who had formerly been a theatrical dresser.
She won't say a word of what he came for, but according to other lodgers in the house he left carrying
a suitcase."

"I see," said Bunch. "He left it in the cloakroom
at Paddington and then he came down here."

"By that time," said Inspector Craddock, "Eccles
and the man who calls himself Edwin Moss were on
his trail. They wanted that suitcase. They saw him get
on the bus. They must have driven out in a car ahead
of him and been waiting for him when he left the
bus."

"And he was murdered?" said Bunch.

"Yes," said Craddock. "He was shot. It was Eccles' revolver, but I rather fancy it was Moss who did
the shooting. Now, Mrs. Harmon, what we want to
know is, where is the suitcase that Walter St. John
actually deposited at Paddington Station?"

Bunch grinned. "I expect Aunt Jane's got it by
now," she said. "Miss Marple, I mean. That was her

plan. She sent a former maid of hers with a suitcase packed with her things to the cloakroom at Paddington and we exchanged tickets. I collected her suitcase and brought it down by train. She seemed to expect that an attempt would be made to get it from me."

It was Inspector Craddock's turn to grin. "So she said when she rang up. I'm driving up to London to see her. Do you want to come, too, Mrs. Harmon?"

"Wel-l," said Bunch, considering. "Wel-l, as a matter of fact, it's very fortunate. I had a toothache last night so I really ought to go to London to see the dentist, oughtn't I?"

"Definitely," said Inspector Craddock . . .

Miss Marple looked from Inspector Craddock's face to the eager face of Bunch Harmon. The suitcase lay on the table. "Of course, I haven't opened it," the old lady said. "I wouldn't dream of doing such a thing till somebody official arrived. Besides," she added, with a demurely mischievous Victorian smile, "it's locked."

"Like to make a guess at what's inside, Miss Marple?" asked the Inspector.

"I should imagine, you know," said Miss Marple, "that it would be Zobeida's theatrical costumes. Would you like a chisel, Inspector?"

The chisel soon did its work. Both women gave a slight gasp as the lid flew up. The sunlight coming through the window lit up what seemed like an inexhaustible treasure of sparkling jewels, red, blue, green, orange.

"Aladdin's Cave," said Miss Marple. "The flashing jewels the girl wore to dance."

"Ah," said Inspector Craddock. "Now, what's so precious about it, do you think, that a man was murdered to get hold of it?"

"She was a shrewd girl, I expect," said Miss Marple thoughtfully. "She's dead, isn't she, Inspector?"

"Yes, died three years ago."

"She had this valuable emerald necklace," said Miss Marple, musingly. "Had the stones taken out of their setting and fastened here and there on her theatrical costume, where everyone would take them for merely colored rhinestones. Then she had a replica made of the real necklace, and that, of course, was what was stolen. No wonder it never came on the market. The thief soon discovered the stones were false."

"Here is an envelope," said Bunch, pulling aside some of the glittering stones.

Inspector Craddock took it from her and extracted two official-looking papers from it. He read aloud, " 'Marriage certificate between Walter Edmund St. John and Mary Moss.' That was Zobeida's real name."

"So they were married," said Miss Marple. "I see."

"What's the other?" asked Bunch.

"A birth certificate of a daughter, Jewel."

"Jewel?" cried Bunch. "Why, of course. Jewel! *Jill!* That's it. I see now why he came to Chipping Cleghorn. *That's* what he was trying to say to me. Jewel. The Mundys, you know. Laburnam Cottage. They look after a little girl for someone. They're devoted to her. She's been like their own granddaughter. Yes, I remember now, her name *was* Jewel, only, of course, they call her Jill.

"Mrs. Mundy had a stroke about a week ago, and the old man's been very ill with pneumonia. They were both going to go to the Infirmary. I've been trying hard to find a good home for Jill somewhere. I didn't want her taken away to an institution.

"I suppose her father heard about it in prison and he managed to break away and get hold of this suitcase from the old dresser he or his wife left it with. I suppose if the jewels really belonged to her mother, they can be used for the child now."

"I should imagine so, Mrs. Harmon. *If* they're here."

"Oh, they'll be here all right," said Miss Marple cheerfully . . .

"Thank goodness you're back, dear," said the Reverend Julian Harmon, greeting his wife with affection and a sigh of content. "Mrs. Burt always tries to do her best when you're away, but she really gave me some *very* peculiar fishcakes for lunch. I didn't want to hurt her feelings so I gave them to Tiglash Pileser, but even *he* wouldn't eat them so I had to throw them out of the window."

"Tiglash Pileser," said Bunch, stroking the Vicarage cat, who was purring against her knee, "is *very* particular about what fish he eats. I often tell him he's got a proud stomach!"

"And your tooth, dear? Did you have it seen to?"

"Yes," said Bunch. "It didn't hurt much, and I went to see Aunt Jane again, too . . ."

"Dear old thing," said Julian. "I hope she's not failing at all."

"Not in the least," said Bunch, with a grin.

The following morning Bunch took a fresh supply of chrysanthemums to the church. The sun was once more pouring through the East window, and Bunch stood in the jeweled light on the chancel steps. She said very softly under her breath, "Your little girl will be all right. *I'll* see that she is. I promise."

Then she tidied up the church, slipped into a pew and knelt for a few moments to say her prayers before returning to the Vicarage to attack the piled up chores of two neglected days.

AGATHA CHRISTIE

Mystery's #1 Bestseller!

"One of the most imaginative and fertile plot creators of all time!"
—Ellery Queen

Agatha Christie is the world's most brilliant and most famous mystery writer, as well as one of the greatest storytellers of all time. And now, Berkley presents a mystery lover's paradise—35 classics from this unsurpassed Queen of Mystery.

"Agatha Christie...what more could a mystery addict desire?"
—The New York Times